QUEEN OF SKIES

KINGDOM OF F

ANNE STRYKER

J A ARMITAGE

Edited By Rose Lipscomb

Cover by Enchanted Quill Press

Proof Reader: Tina Merritt

❀ Created with Vellum

KINGDOM OF FAIRYTALES

You all know the fairytales, the stories that always have the happy ending. But what happens after all those storybook characters get what they wanted? Is it really a happily ever after?

In this prequel, you will find out what happens next, be transported back to those lands you fell in love with and be prepared to meet some new characters along the way.

Kingdom of Fairytales is a new way of reading with one chapter a day and one book a week throughout the year beginning January 1st

Lighting-fast reads you won't be able to put down

Read in real time as each chapter follows a day in the life of a character throughout the entire year, with each bite-sized episode representing a week in the life of our hero.

Each character's story wrapped up at the end of every season with a brand new character and story featured in each season.

Fantasy has never been so epic!

READING ORDER

Kingdom of Fairytales is a 52 book series split into thirteen seasons. Each season has a four book story arc of a fairytale character with the last season seeing them all coming together. You can read any series first with the exception of thirteen, however it is recommended that you read in the order below...

PREQUEL

SLEEPING BEAUTY

1. Queen of Dragons
2. Heiress of Embers
3. Throne of Fury
4. Goddess of Flames

LITTLE MERMAID

5. Queen of Mermaids
6. Heiress of the Sea

7. Throne of Change
8. Goddess of Water

RED RIDING HOOD

9. King of Wolves
10. Heir of the Curse
11. Throne of Night
12. God of Shifters

RAPUNZEL

13. King of Devotion
14. Heir of Thorns
15. Throne of Enchantment
16. God of Loyalty

RUMPELSTILTSKIN

17. Queen of Unicorns
18. Heiress of Gold
19. Throne of Sacrifice
20. Goddess of Loss

BEAUTY AND THE BEAST

21. King of Beasts
22. Heir of Beauty
23. Throne of Betrayal
24. God of Illusion

ALADDIN

25. Queen of the Sun
26. Heiress of Shadows
27. Throne of the Phoenix

28. Goddess of Fire

CINDERELLA

29. Queen of Song
30. Heiress of Melody
31. Throne of Symphony
32. Goddess of Harmony

ALICE IN WONDERLAND

33. Queen of Clockwork
34. Heiress of Delusion
35. Throne of Cards
36. Goddess of Hearts

WIZARD OF OZ

37. King of Traitors
38. Heir of Fugitives
39. Throne of Emeralds
40. God of Storms

SNOW WHITE

41. Queen of Reflections
42. Heiress of Mirrors
43. Throne of Wands
44. Goddess of Magic

PETER PAN

45. Queen of Skies
46. Heiress of Stars
47. Throne of Feathers
48. Goddess of Air

URBIS

URBIS PRISON
BADALAH
DESERT
KISBU
DRACONIS
ZHORE
SHIPLEY
THE VALE
AZREN
ELDER
MOSA
ABORIA
AZURE
ENCHANTIA
URBIS
AIRE
EMERALD CITY
OZ
SKYLA
FLORIS
TULIS
W
E
S
THE FORGE
ARCADIA
RENAIS
MELFALL
ATLANTICE
ANTLA
KINGDOM
OF
FAIRYTALES

4TH NOVEMBER

The leaf shone, catching the light on its way to the forest floor. I spotted it from several yards away and watched it drift, skating from side to side, reluctant to fall. My heart skipped, and I ran to it before its slow descent was complete. Swiping the large, ballooned leaf from the air, I shifted the satchel at my waist and slipped out a small pouch half-filled with pixie dust.

The dust clinging to the leaf was minuscule, but it added to my modest store. The leaves and the trees of Skyla, in fact, the entire island, needed to be coated in the stuff to remain afloat. I just needed a sprinkle of magic, a mere dash. Coupled with enough faith, the magical dust would keep me afloat as well. That, in turn, enabled me to fly. How long it lasted depended on how much I used. The faith part was no problem. As my best friend Whisper said, I had faith for days.

Dropping the leaf, and closing my pouch, I plucked

my knife from the sheath around my thigh, tossed it in the air, and caught the handle on its way down. The perfectly balanced blade sang through the wind when I threw it across the forest into a knot on a far tree.

I grinned when I heard the melody of the discussion of a group of fairies as they conversed with their language of chimes. Following the melody, I plodded on. The job of collecting the dust continued. It was repeated until it grew dull. I had forgotten which way I'd come from, where I wanted to go, and what I wanted to do. Being half-lost was perhaps the only thrilling part of the entire episode because I had the security of knowing I was never fully lost. I could always climb a tree and see my way or ask a pixie to point me in the right direction.

Dozens and dozens, dare I say *hundreds*, of vacant floating islands surrounded Skyla's mainland, most only accessible by using dust to fly to them. Some were large enough to get lost on and others, small enough to hold only a single pixie oak. I spent my days exploring the islands, tossing my knife, and collecting dust. Since I was utterly forbidden to leave Skyla, it was all I could do to stay sane.

With a sigh, I threw my knife nowhere in particular. It skimmed between trees, and my heart leaped as it fled from my sight. A sudden bout of panic overwhelmed me. Peter had given me that knife. I'd had it since I was a child. He'd trained me with it.

I pounded over dead leaves, my moccasined feet finding the hard ground and never slipping. Desperate for a glimpse of the glittering blue of the sapphire-encrusted hilt, my gaze roamed the greens and browns of the forest. Light winked off the gems at a distance, and I drew a deep breath, ease rushing through me.

"That's enough excitement for the day, Lyric," I mumbled to myself, approaching the spot where my blade had landed true. "You'll give yourself a heart attack."

Before I clasped my knife, I noticed the barest sliver of a silver string dangling from it—pixie floss. There was no way I could have known it was there unless I was this close. Pulling my knife free, I lifted the sheer, thin thread dangling from somewhere above me that had been tied off just below where my knife had struck.

The sun lit the canopy as I peered up, trying to find the rest of the string. Pixies zipped from place to place, little more than cheery blips. But their distraction was hardly the reason I couldn't locate the floss's origin. It was too fine. I needed to be up there.

Exhaling, I slipped the long blade of my knife back into its sheath on my thigh. Then I lifted myself up into the tree, shimmying out onto a branch and holding myself steady with the trunk. My ears rang with the pixies' voices as they crowded me, each with something to say, some red-faced and upset I had entered the vicinity of their homes.

"Easy," I said. "I'm a friend of Peter's."

Their eyes went wide for a moment, then they gasped and cooed, delving into my blazing orange hair like it was some telltale sign. I had no idea how every pixie I'd ever met knew Peter. But that was consistently the case, no matter how far I went from the mainland

and Aire, the capital City of Skyla. Maybe the legend of his adventures had spread to even the pixies he'd never met. Of everyone on Skyla—maybe in all the kingdoms—he was the only person who could speak with the pixies in their language. However, I thought it was somehow more likely he knew every pixie personally. I wouldn't put the impossible past him.

"Can you help me?" I asked, figuring they weren't going to settle any time soon.

A pixie with brilliant pink hair stopped in front of my face and tilted her head. Her brows were pinched, and her eyes guarded, and she watched me intently. Pixies didn't share their dust with just anyone, and that was what most humans wanted from them.

"There's some pixie floss tied down there. I think I cut it by mistake. Do you know anything about it?" Hurriedly, I added, "If I've broken something, I want to fix it before I continue exploring."

Pixies, though temperamental and vibrant in every emotion, were generally very polite creatures.

The pink-haired one eased, smiled, and chimed something. The stir around me and in my hair settled a moment to gather replies. When the conversation stopped, she waved me on, out across the branch, and through the tree canopy.

I followed, struggling to keep up as the branch narrowed and bent beneath my weight. Looking back, the pixie zipped over, showering me in dust. My heart lightened with the rare but familiar touch of fresh magic skating over my skin. The feel of the branch disappeared. Nothing but air to hold me now.

My elation didn't appear to amuse the pixie, and she

rolled her eyes before holding up a finger, chiding me, and likely instructing me on how little dust she'd provided, how short a time I'd be able to fly, and how I should follow her quickly. She'd led me just two trees over when the lightness slipped away, lowering me onto a branch.

She pointed down, and I followed the direction of her motion. There, lying across a branch, was a limp thread trailing farther into the distance. My eyes widened. "So it isn't yours? The pixies, I mean?"

Her head shook.

I peered at the thread, the taste of adventure on the tip of my tongue. "Thank you."

Nodding, she grinned and zipped away.

By now, the information that I was related to Peter had swept the entire island, so as I made my way over the branches, following the thread wherever it would lead, pixies dove past me, ogled my hair, gazed at my brown eyes, and laughed. I offered smiles, sighing to think what they must make of me. True, Peter had raised me—as weird as that seemed the older I got and the younger he stayed—but no blood connected us despite the resemblance.

Abandoned as a baby, I'd been told a woman had given me to him as a good luck charm for Skyla. Earlier in my life, I had wanted to know everything about the woman who may have been my mother, but Peter could only scratch his head, peer at the ceiling, and nod that she was beautiful, definitely beautiful. Even that detail had faded from his memory now. The one thing connected to my delivery that he hadn't forgotten was the fact I was Skyla's good luck charm. And that curse had followed me eighteen years, forbidding me from seeing the world with my best friend, Whisper.

An ember of sadness swelled in my chest, burning. I lived for Peter's stories of when he left on adventures. I lived for moments like this when I followed what was likely a discarded trail of thread through the treetops and told myself it was some huge mystery I had to solve.

Afternoon crept by overhead, and I winced. This was useless. I'd be better off heading back to the mainland and helping Tiger Lily with the shop. Prying my gaze from the branch before me, I looked straight ahead.

Everything in me stilled, consumed with a bursting excitement. Nestled a single tree away, was an elegant house with a sloping, dark roof and several feet of a wrap-around porch. It sat amidst the quiet canopy, no pixies troubling it.

My mouth remained agape. I had never come across a home anywhere but in Aire and the three residential bridged islands connected to it. Hell, I had never seen a house in the trees before. The trees were sacredly the pixies' home. Sometimes they didn't mind if you visited. If they liked you well enough, you could stick around for quite a while, but I couldn't so much as pluck leaves or shake off fresh dust without disrupting their lives enough to warrant shrill complaints and an onslaught of attacks.

Balancing across the branch I was on, I hopped off onto the porch of the treehouse. The sturdy wood didn't so much as creak with my weight. Glass windows framed the door; broad, slitted blinds obscured the interior. Nosily, I squinted through the barest cracks, but I couldn't make out much of anything other than shadows.

I knocked. I waited. No one appeared.

And yet, it was in perfectly kept condition. Someone lived here, so I couldn't just barge in. Biting my lip, I turned, following the pixie floss the rest of the way to whatever it was tied to. It connected to a rope ladder that spilled out of a square hole in the porch.

"Oops," I whispered. I thought perhaps I had ruined a cleverly concealed trail to a secret hide-away. My lip chewing transformed into guilty gnawing. Whoever was out here didn't want to be found. Like. At all.

Ashamed, I had to apologize.

Plopping my ass down and dangling my legs out of the hole, I settled in for a late lunch. Eating the two pheasant sandwiches and pear I'd brought with me in my satchel stretched out for a good thirty minutes, but still, no one appeared.

I lay back against the porch, staring at the upside-down wooden house, wondering what secrets it held. Discovering hidden alcoves or giant, gnarled climbing trees were one thing, but to stumble upon something another human had made? That really was an adventure just waiting to be peeled apart.

My fingers skimmed over the sheath at my thigh. People who didn't want to be found had things to hide. Would they be dangerous? Maybe a long-lost pirate from the stories surrounding Peter's favorite trophy—a massive ship dubbed the Jolly Roger. As the story went, he'd flown it up from the sea and landed it on a small island near the mainland after defeating a most fearsome of captains.

"Ah, but none are as fearsome a captain as I, right, Lyric?" I could picture his bright brown eyes and wicked grin as I murmured his words. I ate those moments up, those moments when he'd drag me into his stories as if I had been there, fighting beside him. He'd plop a pirate hat on my head, tip it down, then get serious. Something Peter rarely got to enjoy. *It's because of you we defeated those pirates. Skyla's lucky charm.* By the time I had fixed the hat so I could see, he was back to normal, puffing his chest and claiming that he'd only ever share such credit with me. Most times, he could vanquish a thousand foes on his own, he would claim. "Must've been sick that day," I mimicked his exact words, then snorted, picturing him sniff and drift flawlessly into another tale.

Reminiscing and staring at the house led me into an hour of waiting, but my patience wore thin. "What are you doing?" I snapped at the quiet wood's owner. "Having a party somewhere? Hermits aren't supposed to…party."

My heart stopped.

The party. Whisper's birthday party. I promised her I'd meet her and help plan it today. An hour ago. Maybe longer.

A coarse word bubbled out of my throat as I shot upright, dug into my bag for my gloves, then took hold of the ladder. I slid the whole way to the ground, hitting it with a force that rattled my legs.

"Pardon me!" I called up to the trees. The pixies had been absent around the house, but I hoped one would hear me now. "I'm sorry to bother you! Could anyone point me toward Aire?"

The zipping lights paused, a soft buzz surrounding the area, then in unison they directed me right.

"Thank you so much!" The gratitude barely had a chance to escape before I was running, praying to the great airwoman in the skies that Whisper would find it in her heart not to kill me.

Whisper's hide-brown eyes stared at me, anything but the theme of her party on her mind. Her brow quirked. It dropped again. Her pink lips pursed, then eased. She raised a delicate finger to her cheek and tapped the dark skin with the most precise motions I had ever witnessed.

"I said I was painfully and tragically sorry."

"Hmm?" The syllable stretched. "I know. I forgive you, silly. What's an hour anyway, if not enough time to fall in love with a mysterious stranger deep in the woods? Perhaps some lone boy who also takes to adventuring the outer isles. Quiet. Strong. Enchanting in the *best* way." Her hands clasped, a tiny sigh adding to the dreamy glaze her eyes had adopted. It all shattered. "I mean, why else would you have forgotten this, the most important party I shall ever have?"

As she had said for her tenth, thirteenth, and sixteenth in turn. Nineteen was hardly a special number, but at this party was when she and her true love would finally begin their happily ever after—or so she had decided, all on her own.

I offered a bashful smile, her mock guilt trip hiding the deeper knowledge spinning in her head. She knew something had happened that I wasn't telling her. She knew it likely didn't involve some magical romantic fantasy, but she wished it did, if only a little.

"I just lost track of time," I half-lied. My heart pinched when the deeper glimpse of hurt blinked across her face. I normally told her everything. I didn't know why this was special. A mix of the possibility it could be dangerous and the feeling it was my first real adventure? She had had her adventures.

When she was younger before her Vale father had abandoned her and her mother, Tiger Lily, she had visited the nearby country countless times on family vacations I was forbidden from participating in, no matter how much I begged.

This was *my* adventure.

The idea of how selfish that sounded nearly forced me to blurt everything about the pixie floss path and the treehouse, but she gasped, shaking off the sorrow like it had never been.

"A night to remember." Her hands splayed in front of her and parted as she looked off somewhere in the distance, past the ceiling of her house. "Just think of it, Lyly. A starry sky stretching above us. Lantern light accompanying a roaring fire."

My guilt eased, and I smirked, leaning forward and resting my elbows on the table. I settled my head into my palms. "Adam's arms curled around you beneath a tree canopy laced with pixie floss and paper charms."

Her eyes went wide, only a hint of flush upon her dark skin. She shook her head, wild blond curls flailing as she surveyed the quiet house for unwelcome ears. Leaning close, she grinned. "Oh, that is perfect. You know Mom is making me a special dress. This will be *the* moment for him to see me and fall desperately in love."

I snickered. I wasn't sure about all that, but I did like Adam. The shy boy lived alone, tending to the silk moths past the goat farms, gathering and weaving cloth while making sure the populations didn't grow past what our modest country could handle. The tree leaves were what kept us afloat, after all, and silk moth larvae thought they were delicious. Whisper fell the moment she saw him, dozens of pure white wings flitting about his "ethereal form," as she'd relayed. He was her moth prince. And I couldn't be happier for her.

However, last I heard, he was oblivious to her affections, and she was determined he would be the one to confess his undying love first. Like in a fairytale.

"Life's not a fairytale, Whisper," I chided. Her face morphed into distaste, her nose scrunching. I continued, "If you want something to happen, you have to take the first step on the adventure. So here's what you do when he sees you wearing your fancy dress made with silk from his very own swarm—"

"Kaleidoscope," she chirped. "Call them a kaleidoscope. It's the proper term, after all. You know that. I told you."

My eyes rolled, but I obliged. "Fine. When he sees you wearing silk made from his very own *kaleidoscope*, you sashay up to him, flutter your big, beautiful, brown eyes, then lean close and coo, 'You helped make this dress. Why don't you help me take it off?'"

Whisper gasped. "That is wicked. Positively wicked." She hid a smile that claimed she wasn't entirely against the idea behind her hand, but the expression tipped toward impishness. "But do tell me, how many successful romantic engagements have you partaken of?"

I harrumphed. "Using your proper voice now? Why don't you throw a couple more big words into that sentence?" Every crush I'd ever had ended in failure. I was always too insecure or too late or too boyish or too absent-minded or too *something*. It was always something, and I was never enough.

"I'm sorry, Lyly," she breathed before I realized my smile had dropped off the edge of an island. "I didn't mean anything by that."

"I know. I just…" Shrugging, I sighed. "You have to get your moth prince so I can live vicariously through you, all right? For alas, like Peter, I am doomed to a life of adventure, skirting love like the cooties would kill me."

"Heaven praise the airwoman." Whisper patted my cheek. "You are not forever twelve. You'll have your romance. *You are enough*."

I slipped down until my head could rest in the cradle of my folded arms. Whisper always knew what to say. "I love you, you know that, right? That's my romance."

"Of course." She chuckled, collapsing against the table as well. "And I will never abandon you."

Her hand held tight to mine, and I squeezed it, completing the dumb mantra we had started shortly after her father had gone. "We will never be apart."

She knew how much I wanted to leave. She was the only one who knew I was collecting dust to do so, and she said—no matter what, be it a lover or family or the whole of Skyla—she was coming with me so I would never have to be alone.

Our friendship was my fairytale when I worried about not being good enough, when I worried that the only special thing about me was a "luckiness" I didn't control and barely believed existed. When I remembered that not even my parents wanted me, she reminded me someone did. Not because I was lucky, just because I was me.

And I needed that reminder a lot.

"And that's when we release the white doves." I laughed. We had been planning Whisper's party for hours, snacking on the grilled cheese sandwiches Tiger Lily had made for us when she came home. I had half of one left.

Whisper shoved my arm, correcting me, "White moths."

Adamant, I shook my head. "No, that'll be at the wedding."

"One party at a time! Besides, we already planned my wedding back when we were seven."

My mind drifted back to the tedious scribbles we'd etched together of the two happiest days of our lives. I don't know where my doodles had found themselves, but I was dead sure Whisper still had hers. "If your wedding doesn't have copious amounts of moths, the plan needs revision."

"You think it's hilarious Adam takes care of moths."

"I think it's priceless his official title in the records is 'Silk Moth Babysitter,' yes."

"I should never have told you that."

My stomach hurt holding in so many giggles. "Oh, no. You definitely did the right thing in sharing such valuable information with me."

She tipped up her chin and peered down her nose. "This is the last time such valuable information will ever cross your ears, madam."

I munched my sandwich. "No, it's not."

"No, it's not." She sighed, her eyes shifting behind me to the window. Her smile fell. "Lyly, I think it might almost be midnight."

"What?" I spun, staring outside. The waning moon gleamed back at me, boasting of hours well past ten. "Peter is going to kill me." Stuffing the rest of my sandwich in my mouth, I pushed out of the chair and looked around for wherever my bag had ended up. Not under the table. The other chairs? No. I frantically ruffled my hair. "Killed by a twelve-year-old, the humiliation!"

Sighing, Whisper stood, holding out my satchel after plucking it off the floor beneath my chair. "You really need to talk to him. You'll be nineteen next month. A ten o'clock curfew is a little…restricting."

I took the bag and scoffed. "Tell me about it. But, I mean, he worries. And it's not like he can wait up for very long."

"The ageless twelve-year-old, defeated by the after dark."

My lips spread. I could hardly count the number of times Peter had worn me out with all-night expeditions, parties, full moon swims. When I survived till morning, we'd greet the rising sun with a crow. "It's not the after dark. It's the waiting. He's useless for it. Pretty sure it gives him hives."

Whisper laughed, the bubbly sound like a skipping brook. "Okay, fine. Off with you then." She extended her pinky, and I linked mine around it before pressing my forehead against hers in our classic farewell. I didn't know what was with us and our rituals, but the consistency was reassuring.

"I'll probably see you sometime tomorrow, if an enthralling stranger doesn't whisk me away."

"Excuse you." We parted, and she stared me down. "*Especially* if an enthralling stranger whisks you away. I will need the details immediately succeeding said whisking."

"Bearing that in mind, away I go."

She walked me to the door and leaned against the jam as I exited, calling, with no regard for the neighbors, "Love you!"

"Love you too!" I waved, capturing her grin in the moment prior to her shutting the door. She was a light. And as I wandered into the dark, chilled woods—every treetop gleaming silver as dust-coated foliage reflected moonlight—I needed to hold onto her brightness.

On a scale of one to definitely, how likely was Peter to kill me?

Probably one? Hopefully one? Maybe one…

I picked up the pace, locating our secret underground home deep in the woods on a smaller island past Aire's marketplace and the residential island where Whisper lived. Peering around as I'd always been taught, I checked for anyone who may be lurking then ducked into the hollow trunk entrance when I was sure only the whistling wind would know.

Pushing aside the animal fur that separated the entrance from the main room, I girded myself for…a sleeping Peter. All the air left my lungs when I spotted the fiery-haired boy out cold in his chair. Tinkerbell rested on his shoulder, curled up cheerfully.

All tension easing away, I approached and ruffled the orange locks peeking out beneath his hat. He didn't so much as twitch. I whispered, "I'm home safe," then I lifted Tink off his shoulder. She, unlike him, did stir, blinking groggily at me before frowning.

A pissy chime fell sharp on my ears.

"I know I'm late," I replied quietly. "I'm sorry."

The little pixie sighed and pouted. She patted my hand, content to curl back up once I'd set her in her house. Next, I found a blanket Tiger Lily had made for us and wrapped it around Peter. "We're a weird pair, aren't we?" I murmured, listening to the Lost Boys snore in their bedroom. Father, brother, friend, and child all in one and almost never only one at a time. He could be frustrating, as hot-headed as me, but even our countless squabbles hadn't dashed our bond yet.

Daughter of Pan, that's what the pixies call you. Imagine that. I'm a father. His grins seared my mind, always crystal clear in low points when I needed them most. To everyone on the islands, he was our fearless leader. Respected despite his appearance. All knew how ancient he was though none knew how he had come to be so.

"Night, Peter," I murmured, crossing the room to my

private quarters. As the only girl in the house, the addition had been made just for me not long ago.

When I had readied myself for bed, I collapsed into the padded mattress and furs, curling into the silken sheets. Tomorrow, I'd return to the house in the forest. Wait all day if I had to.

Whoever appeared, friend or foe, I'd be ready for them.

5TH NOVEMBER

As per usual, I woke up first. Birdcalls drifted into my room, announcing the start of a clear morning, and I fumbled to turn on the oil lamp by my bed. At night, a light glow illuminated the rooms thanks to large enchanted bulbs that clung to the ceiling, but during the day, the blue-green hue felt dim.

I supposed lack of light was something the treehouse person didn't have to worry about. Living in a treehouse would be so much nicer than living in this root house, but secrecy was a game Peter particularly liked.

My eyes snapped wide open, all sleepiness shaken. *People who didn't want to be found had something to hide.* A dry laugh escaped before I could dwell on that thought. "No, duh. A forever twelve-year-old obviously has, oh, I don't know, a massive secret about eternal life to hide." Thing was, neither Peter nor the Lost Boys remembered the secret about their youth. And at least for Peter, that bothered him. If he didn't remember how it happened, he couldn't know where to start to reverse it.

There are stories about The Boy Who Never Grew Up, Lyric. They're tales of adventure and wonder and so many fun things, but they overlook the fact that on some quiet nights, when the world is passing by at a rapid speed, the boy wants desperately *to grow up, join it.* The memory put a sick taste in my mouth as I got dressed. I don't remember how many years ago he had told me this, and he only told me once, but it vividly broke my heart each time I recalled. I was little, little enough that he appeared big. My eyes were wide, my lips parted in awe. He patted my head, his brown gaze meeting mine, the only difference being that my irises were ringed in gold. The saddest smile I'd ever seen him wear had crossed his face. *That's why, in the end, I forget. I hate endings, so it's better if they never had beginnings, if I pretend they never were.*

Maybe even he didn't get the message he'd put in my mind then, but I heard it all too clearly. In my end, in Tiger Lily's, in Tinkerbell's, we would all be forgotten. Because if he cared about something, if he cared about us, we were too painful to remember, and if he didn't, some adventure would put us from his head all the quicker.

Haunted by dark thoughts on such a cheerful morning, I exited my room with my bag at my side and puffed my cheeks full of air. Crossing the room, I headed for our food storage and sifted through the fresh fruit, nudging aside the less-than-fresh fruit.

A harsh jab in the face made air pour from my mouth, and I whipped toward the offender, holding an apple close to my chest like it could save me.

Peter's frown and extended finger greeted me. "You

were home late," he accused. "Tink says so late it was nearly today."

I stared down at him. "I was with Whisper, helping plan her birthday party, and lost track of time."

"Whisper…?" A confused brow rose.

"Whispering Meadow. Tiger Lily's daughter. My best friend." Every time I mentioned her, it seemed I had to go through the same reminder. It hurt to know such huge pieces of my life were forgettable. How long could I hope to last in his mind after I was gone? A day or two?

"Oh, Tiger Lily's kid. Still…"—his arms folded—"if anything happened to you…"

"I know," I snapped. His tone, his posture, his expression, *something* about it all pinched a nerve. "Skyla would be doomed. But don't you think I'm a little too old now to have a curfew? I can take care of myself. I'm going to be nineteen next month and—"

"And I need to make sure you stay safe, for everyone's sake. Try not to act so childish."

I flinched, my nails biting into the apple until juice bled over the fruit. "*Childish*? *Me*? Have you looked in the mirror lately, Peter? Not even. Have you seen your bedroom? It looks like a tornado of slingshots and dress-up exploded in there! And when was the last time you bathed properly? If someone isn't reminding you, do you even change your socks? I know you don't. Don't you dare accuse *me* of being childish."

"Lyric!" he complained, his voice pitching. His feet left the ground as he hovered at my height. Despite Tinkerbell still being in her house, Peter always had pixie dust clinging to him—another telltale sign he hadn't bathed properly for a while. "I'm looking out for you and everyone on these islands!"

I shoved the apple in my bag. "I'm just saying, I'm an adult. I shouldn't have to report back to a preteen when I come home a little late. Honest to the great airwoman, Peter, I can't even tell you what others my age spend their nights doing."

His face reddened, apparently less oblivious than I thought. His voice was softer when he spoke again. "I have to keep you safe. I have to know you're safe each day, especially right now."

"And yet when you go off on adventures all over the world, it's good enough to leave me with Tiger Lily, who—for your information—doesn't give me a curfew at all. Is it so much to ask for at least the freedom I can have while trapped here?"

He ran his fingers back through his hair, paused, and looked behind him. His usual green hat rested on the floor, so he skipped over to it and snatched it up.

I took the moment to head toward the exit.

"Where are you going?"

"None of your business."

"It is." He planted his hands on his hips. "What's gotten into you?"

"Nothing." I clenched my bag strap. "Nothing you'd understand anyway. I'm just growing up. That's all."

Silence thickened the air, and it was heavy with everything I hated to feel. When he spoke again, the words were steady, sad. "Which island are you exploring today? I need to know in case something happens and I need to find you."

I pushed aside the furs that covered the exit. Swallowing everything but stubbornness, I mumbled, "I can take care of myself," then I left.

Guilt. Bitter guilt coated me like a layer of cement. It weighed down my actions as I trudged through the bustling market, perusing stalls and greeting acquaintances. I couldn't risk heading back to the treehouse island now. If Peter followed me there in the name of making sure he knew where I was and that I was okay, he'd learn my secret, and if he thought the same thing I did—that someone dangerous possibly lived there—he'd forbid me from discovering the mystery on my own.

He might not forbid my being a part of it. In fact, I was nearly certain he, the Lost Boys, and I would all stake it out and play games in the area until glorious battle or interrogation commenced. But *this was my adventure*. Sidestepping an oncoming rush of people, I ducked beneath the shade of a covered booth and mumbled a curse beneath my breath.

I was being selfish again. Just hurting Whisper wasn't enough for me. Oh no. I had to stab the kid in the back who had taken responsibility for me since my abandonment.

"Lyric?" Tiger Lily's voice yanked my attention from my thoughts. The woman sat in the center of her booth —and how had I missed that this was her booth? Concern rippled through her brown eyes, her dark hair pulled over her shoulder in a single thick braid. "Is everything all right?" Before I could reply, she patted the ground beside her.

My whole body sagged, the cement cracking off as I

went to her and plopped down on her hand-woven rug. “I had a fight with Peter.”

She hummed, wrapping me in her arms. Her cool brown skin sapped everything negative away like magic. Unlike Peter, Tiger Lily remembered when I was a baby and told me stories about how I grew up. Peter, being—well—Peter, didn’t know how to care for an infant. I would have starved had Tiger Lily not discovered my existence and had only just given birth to Whisper. Like sisters, we breastfed beside one another. The woman was the closest thing I had to a mother.

“Can you talk to him?” I asked. “He doesn’t understand that I’m growing up.”

“I imagine he does but rather doesn’t want to admit it.” Tiger Lily cupped my chin and looked into my eyes. The depths there made me swallow, and I remembered she had been an orphan beside Peter when she was his apparent age, and her parents died at the hands of pirates. They were close. They fought together. She grew up. “There are a lot of things Peter doesn’t admit to himself because they hurt, and he’s too young to understand hurt. Ancient, fearless, clever, respected above any here as our leader, and yet so very young. We must protect him while he thinks he’s protecting us.”

Tears burned in my eyes, so I looked away, swallowing a lump in my throat that threatened to choke me. “I’m sorry, Tiger Lily.”

Her head shook. “If you believe you’ve said something to warrant an apology, it isn’t me who needs to hear it. Peter is stubborn, but he isn’t unreasonable. He dwells. And he cares.”

I knew that. I knew that because staring at Peter was

like staring at the person I wanted to be; we were so alike and so different all at once. Taking a deep breath, I wiped my eyes and stood. “Thanks.”

She nodded, smiling as I left.

Exiting into the crowd, I turned myself toward home, fully intent on making peace and making him see reason, but a cloaked figure caught my eye. Shifting on the sidelines, a broad, concealed man strode toward me, passing with uncomfortable speed. My gaze tracked him, and my brow furrowed.

A chill of unease skittered down my spine, whispering on the wind, so I touched the sapphire hilt of my knife and followed him at a distance. He never paused. Could this be the person who lived in the treehouse? No. That island rested past my home, and no bridge connected to it; it was rare that an adult could fly, and we were headed in the opposite direction.

He tore from the crowds, entering the trees, and—he was heading toward the bridge that led to the Jolly Roger. My stomach jumped as I picked up the pace so I wouldn’t lose him in the woods. The second my foot hit a dry twig, it was over.

His head whipped toward me, a shadowed sneer just visible beneath his hood. Then, he ran.

I gave chase. “Stop right there!” I yelled. “Who are you?” But conversation was not the stranger’s strong suit. My feet pounded against sparse twigs and dead leaves until we broke out onto the bridge that connected to Peter’s trophy island. The Jolly Roger sat just out of sight beyond the circle of gleaming trees that kept the small island afloat.

My hand closed around my dagger, but I didn’t want

to kill him. I wasn't even sure I could find the stomach to send my blade into his thigh. "Get a grip, Lyric," I spat at myself. I had been raised on Peter's tales of gore. But the price of his youth and the people he'd forgotten also grew like a weed in my skull.

Killing people meant they never came back. Dead people *did not come back*. And unlike Peter, I wouldn't forget. How could I deem myself worthy of taking a life when I didn't even know if I took it justly or not? For all I knew, I was chasing an innocent recluse.

I screamed when we broke out of the trees and into view of the pirate ship, more from frustration than anything else. The man looked back in the same instant I plunged my hand into my satchel and grabbed my apple. My aim held true, and the fruit careened into his forehead, splitting apart. His body tumbled to the ground.

I jumped him. Cramming my feet against his elbows and sitting on his chest, I finally gained the guts to pull my knife free and press it against his neck. I yanked off his hood just as he was coming to. "Who—"

My heart stopped.

Golden teeth pulled in a rancid smile leered at me. The man's stubbled face and oily hair screamed pirate. Or at least he displayed everything I thought a pirate would from Tiger Lily's and Peter's stories.

"W-who are you?" I stammered, wondering if I should draw blood to make a point I wasn't playing any games.

The man's eyes slithered over my body until I felt violated in the worst ways until being this close made me want to dry heave. Something popped in his mouth, and my body tensed. Foam bubbled from his lips, sputtering as he laughed. I scrambled off him, terrified. The foam and sputtering grew worse, his laughter descending into chokes. But they weren't half as horrible as the silence, the stillness, that followed.

The pirate was dead.

Dead.

There was a pirate on Skyla. And he was dead.

Blood hammered in my ears, clouding all rational thought until I wasn't sure what was worse. I only knew one thing as I skidded back and turned to run. Peter had to know about this.

Now.

"PETER!" I practically fell through the entrance, batting aside the fur covering the main room. Panting, I scanned the Lost Boys, catching Peter's raised brow at the head of the table.

Was it already lunchtime?

That didn't matter. "Peter," I repeated, relieved, still scared, and panicked.

He picked some burnt meat off his plate, and I knew they'd been cooking without supervision again. He did that when he was mad; that is, he pretended to be a capable adult. "What is it?" he asked.

"You a'ight?" Slightly asked.

My head could only shake. "Peter, there was a pirate in the market." He went deathly still. "I think… I think…" Bile rose, but I forced my words out. "I think I killed him, Peter. On the trophy island, in front of the

Jolly Roger. He started to foam at the mouth before I knew it, and—"

Peter slammed his hands against the table, startling Tinkerbell as he stood. More than a little anger painted his expression, and I actually shrunk back from the boy. "That's nothing to joke about, Lyric. I know we had an argument this morning, but you don't have to make up stories to prove you can take care of yourself. That's the opposite of maturity." Worry and anger mixed and melded in his eyes.

Everything in me felt run through with an arrow. "I'm not making it up. Peter—"

His eyes hardened.

Tootles's small voice interjected. "You know what the pirates did to us, Lyric."

"I—"

The boys' heads turned away from me, their eyes looking from one to the next. Only Peter's livid gaze clung to my skin. His blaze of anger sparked my own.

"You don't believe me. How can you not believe me!" My fists clenched. "I've never lied to you before!"

"You've never grown up before either!" His shout hung in the air. Even Tinkerbell looked between us, her lips parted. She rose, fluttering in front of him and shaking her head, but he swatted her away. "Adults are lying, sniveling, dangerous things. They only think about themselves, which isn't the best, but I understand. However, the minute they play others to get what they want is the minute they stop being a friend of mine."

My eyes stung. Water dripped down my cheek when I blinked. "Fine," I said, my voice shaking. "Don't believe me and quit being my friend." I forced my legs to move me toward my room, stopping just before I crossed the threshold. "I wish I had a real father. A real father would trust me. Instead, I'm stuck with an insipid child like you."

"Lyric..."

I didn't wait for him to continue. I all but slammed the door and collapsed into bed, crying myself to sleep. Like an adult.

Groggy, I awoke with an urgent need to relieve myself. The flowers on my ceiling glowed over my room, their calming shade doing little to hide the memories that hit me the moment I sat up. Peter hated me now.

Deflated, I wiped my cheeks. Disgusting, crusted tears clung around my eyes, and worse still, I wanted to continue crying. I wanted to scream and scream until my weird little family would curl up around me and make all the dumb things better. Did Peter think I wanted to grow up? Did he think I liked not knowing what I was doing with myself? Did he think I enjoyed the thought of leaving him behind, of attempting to find my own way in this scary, unknown world?

Everything I wanted—adventures, knowledge, purpose—were all his fault. The damn twelve-year-old was all I aspired to be. But my wings had been clipped, trapping me here where nothing happened, where I made adventures out of treehouses and got yelled at when I thought I'd finally found something important.

Or maybe I'd just made things worse. If I hadn't been there, that man would have lived. Peter could have found him, and he would have known what to do better.

He could have information about what the pirate was doing here, how the pirate had even gotten here. Now he had nothing to go on, and because he thought I was lying, he wouldn't even think to look for anything else.

Bracing myself, I grabbed my satchel, sniffed, and peeked out my door. The quiet main room looked back at me, not even Tinkerbell glowing asleep in her house. No snores. No whispers.

I slipped out of my room and into the mild evening on my way to the outhouse. Where was everyone? Thoughts of being abandoned now that I was an adult scathed the edges of my mind, and it took all my power to keep my breaths steady. Something like this wouldn't make Peter abandon me, right? I was still Skyla's good luck charm, wasn't I?

I still had purpose. *Didn't I?*

Gasping, I finished up in the outhouse as quickly as I could, washing my hands in the river faster than I normally did. My feet pounded against the soft earth, set on fleeing to Whisper. She could reassure me. If nothing else, she would tell me I was enough for her, that we'd always be friends, that—

Peter.

His orange hair shone in the distance, moonlight reflecting off the pixie dust dousing it. I stopped beside the entrance to our home, my throat tight. A tear trickled down my cheek as he approached.

Lost in thought, he didn't look up until he was just a few steps away, then he stopped. "Lyric…" The wind caught my name, pulled it away. "Why are you still crying?"

I scrubbed my cheek against my shoulder, but more

tears followed. "I thought… Well, no one was here. I just…" My lip trembled, and I leaned my head back to try and stop the tears.

"Head off to bed, men. We'll talk later."

The Lost Boys hesitated before slipping past us and entering the secret entrance to our home.

When it was just us, Peter sighed, scratching the back of his head. "I'm sorry I yelled at you. You just know that…" He floated toward me, his arms crossed at first, then limp at his sides. "I don't have to tell you what you understand. I'm sorry for yelling. I'm sorry for what I said. You are my friend, Lyric. More than that. Things are just a little odd right now. Something is changing in the air, and I don't like it."

Water blurred my vision, but I numbly recognized Tinkerbell's tiny hands against my cheek, pushing droplets away and soaking herself as she tried to dry my tears. She hugged my face when she realized I just couldn't stop crying. "I'm sorry," I blubbered.

"And about your curfew," he began.

I started to shake my head but didn't want to throw Tinkerbell, so I stopped and whispered, "I don't care about that anymore."

He bumped my shoulder, floating beside me. "Sure, you do. Just maybe not right in this moment when all you can focus on is leaking, like a little girl." Plucking Tinkerbell off my face by her wings, he plopped her into his pocket to dry off, then he removed his hat and used it to dry my tears. "You're smart. We've raised you smart enough to handle yourself. So what if you come back a little late now and again? As long as I know you're safe and sound when the second star sets. Okay?"

"I'm sorry for what I said about a real father."

He shrugged, reclining midair. "You didn't mean it."

Though smiling, I could feel the hurt swirling in his eyes. It stabbed me through the gut. "I could never mean it." I swallowed. "Never." I looked up at the star-spattered sky, and a lightness swelled in my chest. Shifting my satchel around, I pulled my pan flute out. "Can we play in the tree tonight?" It had been so long since we'd played together, watched the stars, and joked about how we ruled the world. The tree was where he'd taught me to play; hell, it was where we'd made my pan flute.

Peter looked at the oak that hid our home beneath it. Massive, it stretched above all the other trees in the area and plateaued near the top, creating a flatbed large enough to stretch out on. When he looked back at me, I knew the answer before he spoke. "I need to talk to the boys tonight, and it's getting late, but you're welcome to stay out for as long as you want. Try…try not to go too far tonight though. Please."

"Is something wrong?" The pirate flashed through my mind, and I paled. "Did you…?"

He shook his head. "Wrong? Of course not. What could possibly go wrong with Skyla's good luck charm around?" Hovering over me, he rustled his hair, showering me in dust. I squinted, hundreds of flecks falling before my eyes. My feet left the ground before I'd really told them to. Peter's grin filled my vision when I met his gaze. "Daughter of Pan." He smirked.

A smile brightened across my face, making me lighter.

"Don't get into any trouble I wouldn't." He stepped

down by the hollow entrance trunk, watching me for confirmation.

I bent my arms at my waist.

The approval on his face before he vanished into our home eased any worries I'd had before. Maybe everything wasn't taken care of just yet, but tomorrow I'd show him the dead pirate if no one else reported it first. We'd figure out where to go from there.

Floating around for a little while, I waited until the last minute the dust would hold me up to settle in the tree, lie back against a branch, and pull my flute from my bag. The low notes filled the night, their lulling tones and warm melody encompassing everything they touched.

Although I don't remember when, the song carried me to sleep.

6TH NOVEMBER

Less than gracefully, I snorted upright, blinking at my surroundings. When had I fallen asleep? My pan flute rested at my side, unharmed, so I brushed it off and glanced through the silver-dusted leaves and branches at the sky to gather the time.

Before I could judge the position of the stars, a humanoid streak flew past them. My breath caught. Fumbling in my bag, I ripped out a homemade spyglass and positioned it at my eye. Sure enough, in the distant sky, a person soared toward Skyla. Was it Peter? But, no, it seemed larger than Peter.

Heart racing, I stood, measuring the person's trajectory. If they kept straight, they'd land on treehouse island. I watched them for several seconds. They continued straight.

I couldn't afford to lose them.

Torn between only just making up with Peter and going against his wishes again, I kept my distressed grunts and grumbles to a minimum as I snagged my pouch of pixie dust from my bag, sprinkled as much as I dared to lose on my head, and whipped out of the tree.

I couldn't lose the person. Even if I didn't wait to confront them until I told Peter, I had to find out if they were another pirate. If they were connected to that house. Gaze narrowed, I darted through the air after them. My dust ran out before I made it all the way, but the second I touched down on that island, I set my hand at my knife and ran toward the treehouse.

All my life, Peter had told me I was the charm protecting Skyla. Maybe this was the moment when I'd actually put work into that title, when my physical efforts would be Skyla's protection.

Close now, I slowed, hiding behind trees and pushing forward, careful to watch my step. When I was certain the house was hidden in the branches just before me, I pressed my back against a large trunk and pulled my blade free. I surveyed everything in front of me first, then to either side. Finding nothing, I glued my gaze to the small clearing beyond the trunk and before the hidden treehouse.

My heart beat erratically, the rhythm a mixture of flying, running, and waiting. What if they found me? They could fly. Like Peter. I'd never seen anyone else fly as high as that. Pixie dust could be fickle, and if you ran out at that height, only a bitter end awaited unless a pixie caught you. I knew. I'd flown so high a number of times, and the pixies were *never* happy when they had to catch me.

Leaves rustled above.

I stopped breathing.

A boy dropped through the canopy, pulling up at the

last second and landing with his back toward me. Muscular arms reached up toward a thick braid of chocolate brown hair. Strong hands pulled the tie free, then his fingers slipped through the starlight-spattered locks. His whole body glimmered in the dappled moonlight.

My mouth opened, tongue going dry.

Murmured, deep, enticing words I couldn't make out sliced through the chirping night. Was he talking to something? A ball of silver light flitted before him, and my eyes bulged. A pixie?

Only Peter... But here this boy—nearly my age if not older—stood, drenched in pixie dust and talking with one *just like Peter*. Who was he? I had to know. I just had to.

I nearly stepped out from behind the tree when his head nodded toward the ladder, and his low murmur continued.

Every blooming curse I knew dredged through my mind. *The. Ladder.*

Darting back to my hiding place, I dropped my knife and missed dodging a stick when I dodged the blade. The loudest *snap* I'd ever heard broke the woods.

The boy's back tightened, tension filling him. I didn't move. My hands clamped against my mouth.

He glanced over his shoulder, a smoldering gaze of mixed greens and browns finding me, widening. Sensual, full lips parted, and his head cocked.

I backstepped, a chorus of curses continuing confidently inside my skull. My foot hit another stick, and the world mocked me as that *crack* echoed. I closed my eyes to wallow in dark embarrassment alone.

"Hello," he said, loud enough for me to hear. "To whom do I owe the pleasure of such a late and unexpected visit?"

My eyes opened, and fear coursed through me. His face had darkened, his eyes pinned on the blade by my feet.

"That's a pirate's knife," he said. He didn't touch the sheath at his waist, but his hand hovered near it. "Who are you?"

All kindness sucked from his melodic voice, my mind shook free of entrancement. I held up my hands. "Lyric. Daughter of Pan." I don't know why I said that, but I glanced at the male pixie, hoping he'd come to my aid like most did. He settled on the boy's shoulder, saying nothing. I inhaled, continuing, "What do you know about pirates?" I looked him over again. He wore a loose linen shirt and dark trousers. The style wasn't unlike most of Skyla's clothes, though his hair was longer than most male residents kept theirs. He didn't look like a pirate. At least, not like the pirate I'd seen yesterday.

"What do I know about pirates? Nothing." He tapped his dagger's hilt, and I realized he had more than one, maybe four or five, on his belt. "But blades are a different story."

My breath hitched when he strode forward, eating the ground between us. He bent in front of me, plucked my knife from the ground, and flipped it to blade-side between his fingers, offering.

"How do you come by a pirate's knife?" he whispered.

My eyes flicked between him and the pixie on his

shoulder. The tiny creature's stare was nearly as severe as his. I clasped the handle, meeting resistance. Quickly, I snatched it from him.

His chin tilted up, and he looked at me with half-lidded eyes.

"My father gave it to me," I answered, sheathing it, but keeping my hand near.

The boy's arms folded. "Was your father a pirate?"

Did they not know of Peter Pan? I sterned my expression. "No. He killed them."

Finally, the pixie chimed, the hushed words said so softly I almost believed I should be able to understand them.

The boy shrugged his free shoulder and turned on his heel. "Skye says you're safe—what was it?—Lyric? Like a song lyric?"

"My father—" It was so weird calling Peter that. He was always Peter to me. "—named me after the words because we call the wind music and those who fly through its song lyrics."

"You fly then?"

"I'm sorry. Who are you?" My thumb touched the sapphire hilt of my knife as my brows lowered. Peter had trained me in one-on-one combat, not that I'd practiced it for a while. I could hit a mark halfway across a forest, but I'd grown rusty in everything else involving a blade. Even cutting vegetables if I were being honest, but I didn't have to be quite that honest with him.

"Bay."

"*Bay?*"

A satirical smile turned up one corner of his lips.

"I'm sorry. I don't have a poetic story to accompany my name. It's just *Bay*."

"Do you live here, just *Bay*?"

"Have you been snooping around my house, Wind Song?"

My cheeks heated, but I frowned. "Not intentionally. There was a freak accident involving a bit of cut pixie floss when I was wandering the forest."

"Was there now?" He lifted off the ground. "Well, thank you for stopping by. Please don't come back. Cheers."

"Hold on right there. Just a minute, sir."

He turned in the air, even his pixie raising a brow at me.

Swallowing, I blurted every thought in my head, "I saw you fly in. Where did you come from? Why are you out here living secretly in the woods? How in the name of the airwoman do you have a pixie with you?"

He stared at me for several moments. "Do you have any other questions, or would you prefer I write you an autobiography of my personal life? In your nosiness, I hope you haven't disorganized my house. Everything was alphabetized."

I glowered at him, and he was lucky I wasn't holding my knife anymore, or it may have shaved off a bit of his hair. "Oh, I'm sorry. Are there actually things in your house? With an attitude that large, I'm surprised you fit at all."

He leaned forward, looking down at me with his arms set akimbo. That dark hair slid over his shoulders like silk. "Cheeky. My apologies. I'm not used to guests grilling me in the middle of the night about every detail of my livelihood." He flipped upside down, and it was becoming the slightest bit clear how a pixie had attached itself to him.

Pixies adored children. Adults lost whatever special thing it was that allowed them to bond and communicate. I don't remember ever having been able to hear their words, but Whisper swore she had, and she missed it. The childish, arrogant person before me was nothing less than a suave Peter, playing a game by toying with me.

My eyes closed briefly because I did *not* just think he was suave.

"What was that first question again?" he prompted, his gaze drifting away. "Oh, wait. I don't want to answer the first one. How about the second one, then? Why I'm living secretly in the woods. That's an easy one." The cheeriness fell away. "I don't like company. Good eve." He floated up onto his porch and yanked the ladder through the hole, closing off the entrance.

I stared up through the trees, barely making out the house's foundation even when a soft yellow light blinked on.

"You're an ass!" I snapped after several minutes of gaping.

"Am I?" he called back. "I'm not the one shouting at someone's house while a hundred pixies are trying to sleep nearby."

He had a point. And it made me want to punch him. Growling, I surveyed the area, found a knotted tree with a good starting hold, and pulled myself up into the bows. Careful to be precise when I entered the treetops, I led myself to his porch and hopped down. The blinds were still closed, but light gleamed through the cracks.

Before I could knock, his door flew open. He stared at me, looked at the bundle of ladder beside my feet, then narrowed his eyes, perhaps, looking for dust. "How did you—"

"You're an ass," I whispered.

His head reeled back, and he blinked, then an odd smile twisted his lips. He leaned against the door jam. "All right, Wind Song. All right. Well played, I'll give you that."

I mockingly held an invisible gown and curtsied.

"But I'm really not this interesting. Just a hermit with a pixie. We can't be that rare. Would you *please,* very politely, go away now?"

"No," I said simply. "It's not normal for people to have pixies and fly in from the stars. You're hiding something, and I need to find out what."

"Is that your job?"

"Well, it certainly isn't Silk Moth Babysitter's…"

He chuckled, the sound deep and smooth like roasted chestnuts. "I swear, if that's a thing…"

"I'll never tell." My eyes drifted over his shoulder to the one-room abode. Tidy yet lived-in, it boasted the same essence I'd gotten from the exterior, except it was filled with incredible things. Books. Papers. Trinkets of all kinds that I'd never seen before. A huge map covered the far wall. My eyes widened.

He glanced over his own shoulder and quirked a brow. "What? Have you never seen a bachelor pad before?"

"Can I look at your map?" The words left my mouth breathless, and I met his gaze.

His lips pinched, but he surprised me. "Sure."

The boy stepped aside, and I forgot that he was a stranger as I entered the enclosed space. His pixie sat off in the corner on a full-sized cot, watching me, but I paid him little mind. My hand stretched toward the intricate etchings, each detail impeccably placed. "You made this?"

"...yeah." He stood beside me, close enough that I could feel heat near my back.

"It's Skyla." I faced him.

His eyes drifted to the calligraphy title, boasting *Skyla*. "How'd you guess?"

"Don't make me hit you."

"You'd hit a man in his own home while he was just minding his business and trying to get to bed?" He placed an offended hand against his heart, playing up a wounded expression.

I elbowed him in the side, remembered he wasn't a friend, then cleared my throat, sidestepping to put distance between us. "I definitely would."

He rubbed his ribs. "A wonder why I don't regularly entertain company."

I looked at the wall above his cot. Another untitled map splayed there, this one dotted with notes. "Where's that?" I asked, approaching it.

"That's elsewhere," he mumbled. "I'm sorry. How rude of me. Would you like a tour?"

"Yep." I grinned. He wasn't exactly frowning, so I looked closer at the map, skimming over the notes

Sirens aren't nixies. Nixies aren't mermaids. Don't be in Skull Rock after dark.

Excitement bubbled in my chest, and I whirled on him. "Tell me your secrets."

"What in the world is wrong with you?"

"Many, many things, Star Boy. Secrets now. Therapy later."

He laughed, and it was full. Shaking his head, he patted my hair. "Calm down. It's late. Scratch that, it is very, very early, and I haven't slept yet."

"It really sounds like you're inviting me back. Are you inviting me back?"

"Regrettably." He smirked. "But only because you've flattered me by ogling my maps." He folded his arms. "Here's the deal: tomorrow night bring an offering of good grace—food, I mean food—and tell no one where I live. I'll tell you some stories, then you can go away, a satiated little monster."

"How do I know you aren't planning to get me alone and jump me?"

He raised a brow, extending his arms to the room.

I glanced at the space in which we were alone and pressed my lips together. "Fair point. How do I know you aren't going to fly off somewhere before I come back, then?"

He scratched his chin. "I suppose you don't. You'll just have to have a little faith and trust when I say I'm sticking around till the tenth."

I held up a pinky. He looked at it, blanking. "You aren't serious."

"Am." I wiggled my pinky.

Sighing, he linked his finger with mine. "If you bring cheese tomorrow, I might forgive you for this."

"Do you mind if it's goat?" I pulled my hand away, trying not to take offense when he wiped his on his shirt.

"I won't be picky."

"Great." I led myself to the door. "Tomorrow then."

"Later today, really."

"Promise you'll be here?" I set my hand on the doorknob.

He shrugged, but it was as good an answer as any. "You said you knew how to fly? Do you need some dust to get back home?"

Skye chirped, the sound a clear protest, so I shook my head. "I always keep a bit on me. As long as I don't fall out of the tree, I should be fine."

"A pity if that did happen." His smirk stretched into a wicked grin.

I rolled my eyes and lowered the rope ladder. Despite his words, he watched me until I made it safely down. Floating just over his porch like a silver ghost in the moonlight, he continued watching until I was out of sight.

My tired mind wandered while I helped Whisper set up the small island grove for her party tomorrow. I had managed a short nap after meeting Bay, but past that, my head refused to quiet down. Questions and mysteries swirled.

When I'd spotted him, he was little more than a shooting star, heading straight down to his home. He hadn't come in from the horizon. He had come from the sky.

A sigh filtered past my lips.

"Okay!" Whisper stopped passing me the next lantern to string in the trees beside our party location on the edge of the island. I looked down from my perch and quirked a brow. She set her arms akimbo. "What is up with you? You don't sigh wistfully. I sigh wistfully. You're a million miles away, and we know you aren't allowed that much traveling time." A grin brightened her soft brown cheeks. "Tell me everything."

"What?" I cleared my throat. "What are you talking about? Everything about what?"

"Let's start with the dark circles under your eyes. Did you sleep at all last night? Or…were you *involved* in something else?" She finally relinquished the lantern and reached for the next while I threaded it in a hammock of glimmering pixie floss. In the late sunlight, the threads gleamed.

"I slept." *Some.*

"You're hiding something." Her lips pulled in a pout. Gaze averting, she handed me the next lantern. "Is it a boy?"

Feigning coolness, I replied, "Not everything is a boy." I feared the heat rising to my cheeks gave me away.

"Definitely a boy." Her sage nod accompanied a wistful sigh, and she was rightfully the queen of those. What was I thinking in allowing myself to encroach upon her domain? Her long lashes fluttered. "Oh, please tell me something about him."

"There's nothing to tell." Trying to change the

subject, I asked, "Do you think I could have some of your mom's goat cheese?"

"Lyly, it's my birthday." The serious undertone to her words almost hid the childish notion. "You shouldn't lie to me on my birthday."

The sick, guilty feeling in my gut boiled, but I had promised to tell no one about him. Or rather. I'd promised to tell no one where he lived. Hopping out of the tree, I grinned. "If there is someone worth mentioning, he'd be my date to your party tomorrow night."

Whisper's eyes bulged, and she clasped my hands. "Yes, this is absolutely true." Before I could get another word in, she squealed. "This is the best gift ever. We'll have to have a joint wedding."

"Oh, so if we are renovating the plans, we must include as many moths as possible, right?"

"You have to stop being so jealous that Adam is a moth prince."

I snickered. "A most regal prince of moths indeed."

She nodded, pressing the last lantern into my hand. "Quite."

"Where are you going?" Peter stopped me before I'd made it far from home. Half a foot off the ground, he hovered, arms folded and brow quirked. Beside him, Tinkerbell flitted, her stance much the same as his.

I diminished my groan and faced his steady brown stare. The white moon sent cool light over us, accentuating the chill in the air. "Out." I moistened my lips. "I'll be back before morning."

His expression hardened. "Are you going far?"

"Not too far." Nowhere in Skyla was particularly far.

He scrutinized me several moments, my stomach tight with worry he'd stop me, but then he sighed. "Okay. You have your knife?"

I brushed the sheath at my thigh, though I doubted it would do me much good if I didn't have the guts to use the blade. "Yeah. Always."

"Be back by morning." Jabbing a finger toward me, he jutted out his chin and narrowed his eyes.

I nodded, trying not to show my elation when he ducked back into the hollow trunk and disappeared down into our home. Breath held, I waited and watched for any sign he might be coming back, but nothing moved.

Turning on my heel, I held my bag close and darted toward Bay's island, only using a smidge of dust each time I needed to cross an un-bridged divide. When a shadowed form entered my vision just before reaching his house, I skidded to a stop. Crouched, the figure seemed to be toiling in the bushes, a silver ball of light sending a soft glow over a defined profile.

All the air in my lungs escaped in a gentle breath.

"Evening, Wind Song," Bay greeted, not bothering to look up.

I noticed the slight curve of his lips deepen, so I smiled to match. "I come bearing bribery."

"Bribery?" He settled back on his haunches, finally gracing me with a look. "Let's see if it's acceptable then."

Skye peered at me, judgment in his tiny eyes when I approached and lifted the flap of my satchel, revealing half a loaf of soft bread, a ball of gooey cheese, and a handful of berries not unlike the ones he had gathered in a basket at his side.

He peeled back the cheesecloth and sniffed the white mound. "It's fresh."

"The goats breed year-round here since the weather is always so temperate." An icy breeze swept through my long hair to spite my words, and my skin prickled in response.

His wry smile set a flurry of butterflies loose in my stomach. I ignored them the best I could.

"Have you ever had blackberry tea?" he asked.

I shook my head.

He plucked the basket off the ground and rose into the air. "A pity. You're missing out."

"Your bad manners can't sway me as long as you tell me your secrets." I followed him when he drifted toward his home, popping berries into his mouth as he went.

"A shame I have no secrets to tell." Before I could protest, he added, "I do, however, have a few stories you might like." He tossed me a berry before soaring into the treetops.

Moments later, the rope ladder dropped before me. Minutes later, we were seated in the center of his house, the floor strewn with dozens of things I'd never seen before. He showed me a real telescope and a golden sextant with elaborate designs. He told me about the mermaids of Atlantis, a genuine scale scintillating between his fingers.

We talked and ate and did, in fact, drink some blackberry tea until, quickly and without my notice, the night slipped into the next day.

7TH NOVEMBER

Bay paused, his knife glinting in the oil lamp light as he twirled it into a sheath on his belt and lowered his hands from the dramatic rendition he was acting out. An odd grin tugged on the corner of his lips. "Close your mouth, Wind Song. Surviving a bear is hardly the highlight of tonight's multi-story event."

"It's not just a bear. You've got sirens after you too." Lying on my stomach, I propped my head in my hands and crossed my ankles.

He twisted, tossing a glance over his shoulder. His eyes widened into massive circles like he had just spotted the winged creatures through the make-believe foliage. "I forgot about them." A muffled curse whispered into the suddenly tense air. Then he pulled his knife again, blocking an invisible blow. His body careened back, narrowly missing the bookshelf as he crashed into the floor. "Don't you dare even try to bewitch me," he struggled to say, clamping a hand above his knife like he was covering the woman's mouth.

Skye's chirping laughter broke the heavy moment, and I glanced at the pixie as he rocked and kicked his legs.

The scene fell away, and Bay deadpanned, floating back to his feet. "You ruined it, Skye."

Chiming responded.

"That is exactly what happened, thank you very much." Bay's eyes rolled in light of Skye's next response. "I did not forget the bear. I fought him off with my third arm, obviously."

"You are significantly less of an ass tonight," I said, flashing him a grin.

He floated into a cross-legged position on the floor. "A miracle the change in a man's character when he's not sleep deprived."

"Uh huh."

He reached over me, snagging a piece of bread from my satchel. "Food helps too."

My cheeks heated. "You still haven't told me where you came from last night, Star Boy."

"I haven't?" He fell back, the piece of bread hanging out of his mouth. "Oops."

"Please?"

"I told you, I have no secrets for you to pry out of me. Just stories, with a side of sarcasm."

I rolled my eyes. "An unnecessary side, really."

"You appreciate it." He swallowed the bread and shot up. "You already know where I came from. The stars. I'm a fallen angel. A little bird just out of my egg."

My brows knitted. "Am I supposed to know what that means?"

He shrugged.

"Do you even know what that means?"

Another shrug. "Should I? Seems entirely unimportant."

Skye flitted over to my bag and ripped a handful of cheese out before plopping onto Bay's head. Bay looked up, trying to see the little creature, then his gaze dropped to me, all childishness gone in an instant. His lips spread in an alluring smirk. "It's your turn, Wind Song."

"What?"

"Tell me a story about one of your adventures."

My heart sank, and I pulled myself up off the floor, hugging my legs close to my chest. "I've never actually left Skyla, so I don't have any adventures to tell."

He scoffed. "You mean to say you know how to scale the pixie oaks, but you've never stumbled upon anything more interesting than my house?"

Casting off the empty sensation filling my stomach, I leaned toward him. "Why, yes. That is exactly what I'm saying. Why do you ask? Should I have?"

"Secrets fill these islands, more than you'd expect. At least, I'm half-certain."

Excitement burbled to the surface. "Show me."

His head shook. "Sadly—for you—that's not how it works. You have to find them yourself, or they have no meaning."

I pouted. "I suppose begging wouldn't do me much good?"

"You know they say that only the innocent and heartless can fly, and I fly better than the best of them."

"Heartlessness. What a thing to be proud of," I grumbled, but I knew that wasn't the real reason we could fly. It wasn't innocence or happy thoughts or youth. It was belief. Belief that you could never abandon. The second you doubted whether or not you could fly was the second you never would be able to again, or so the story went.

I hadn't realized silence encompassed us until he released a breath, murmuring, "I hope the thoughts streaming behind your eyes are a story you'd like to tell me."

"Sorry to disappoint."

"I find it very difficult to believe someone who carries a pirate's knife at her hip has nothing interesting to share." He lifted his cup and swirled the tea, pausing before taking a sip. "Unless you're dressing for the life you want, not the one you have. Are you scared to leave, or are you unable to?"

"That's none of your business." I swallowed the bitterness resting on my tongue and sifted through my bag to find any stray berries. Their sweetness mellowed my unease.

"The last five hours have been none of your business, and yet, I hate to inform you, this is what conversation and getting to know someone looks like."

I frowned. "You've kept your secrets. I won't lie and say I don't have any of my own, but I'm also not going to share them."

His eyes sparkled, the lamplight sending a shimmer across his tan skin. "Can you really fly?"

"Yeah, of course. How else would I get to this remote island?"

"Then why haven't you left Skyla?"

My mouth fell open, and I smacked him. "You tricked me."

"You are violent." But he laughed and fell back again, knocking Skye out of his hair. The little pixie took the tumble in stride, to my surprise floating to sit on my shoulder with his cheese. "Interesting," Bay said, linking his arms under his head. "I guess he's warmed up to you."

"Most pixies are comfortable around me because they know Peter."

"Are you sure that's why?" He kept his gaze on the ceiling.

I blinked. "Yes, of course."

"Hm."

"What?"

"Nothing." His expression turned pensive, hazel eyes drifting toward the unnamed map. "I've enjoyed this." His lips quirked. "Despite your nosiness, rudeness, and violence, it hasn't been horrible."

"That's one hell of a compliment," I noted dryly.

"Yeah."

Calm saturated the air, and I breathed it in, looking out the window. The still-dark sky hinted at the coming dawn, all too soon lightening with gentle blues. "I have to go soon," I murmured.

"Why?" The soft edge to his deep voice sent a chill racing down my spine.

"Because." When the second star moon set, Peter expected me home.

"Why?" he repeated in the same enticing manner.

I scoffed. "How old are you?"

"Not sure." His eyes closed, and I took a moment to

trace the shape of his jaw, the downturn of his mouth, the long, still lashes framing his eyes.

The quietest chime met my ear, and I glanced at Skye to find the most mature expression I'd ever seen on a pixie before. He winked, floating off my shoulder with the last bit of his cheese to settle onto the cot. My cheeks heated, and I pressed my lips together.

Gathering my courage, I said, "Tomorrow night at dusk, my friend is having a birthday party on one of the smaller islands near the mainland."

"Hmm?" He didn't shift.

"Would you like to go? With me?"

"Yeah," he answered. My chest fluttered with the word, unprepared for an added, "It's a date."

Air caught in my throat. His half-lidded gaze fell on me when I didn't reply, then the least childish smile spread across his face. He nodded toward the Skyla map. "Which island?"

I pried my eyes off him to find the location and pointed it out.

"Okay. I'll see you then." His eyes reclosed. Skye chirped, and Bay chuckled. "All right. All right. Would you be so kind as to leave the bread and cheese?"

I looked at the pixie's broad grin and rolled my eyes. "How could I say no to that face?" Lifting the food out of my bag, I set it beside Skye, who spun into the air above my head. Dust showered over me, and my feet were off the ground in an instant.

"Well, what do you know. You really are a lyric in the wind." Unmoved, Bay lit a fire in my chest with nothing but the intense gleam in his eyes. I took a deep breath, attempting to quell the flurries, but they didn't dare settle.

I wasn't a romantic. I wasn't Whisper. I didn't have the confidence she did when it came to love and being loved. But I had enjoyed talking to him tonight. He carried so much adventure and mystery and allure. I wanted to pick him apart for his secrets and then dig deeper, finding what he hid within his soul.

I also wanted to destroy the twinges of pain that came with the knowledge he only stayed till the tenth before disappearing and stealing the magnetism that drew me in.

My toes curled in my moccasins, and I floated over Bay on my way to the door. "I told you I could."

"I did doubt it just a little." His body lifted into the air, pausing upside down and a couple feet off the ground.

I opened his door and smirked. "Because you're an ass."

Arms folded and head shaking, he mumbled, "Good eve, Wind Song."

"Sleep well, Star Boy." Before I stared at his crooked smile for too long, I flew out into the night.

Flying home was far easier than walking, and I made great time, running out of dust just before hitting the last bit of trek through the woods. A mixture of feelings coalesced within me as I collapsed into my bed, ready to sleep away all the hours between now and Whisper's party.

I hardly knew what to do with the wistful sensations. Part of me liked them. Another part was afraid.

Too many risks filled the cracks, and I had no way to know how to bridge them.

So I closed my eyes and tried to set aside my crush before it could morph into something far, far more dangerous and unknown and…sweet.

8TH NOVEMBER

The grove was alive with motion and brightness, even in the dusk. Pixie floss gleamed silver and gold, thanks to the moonlight and lantern light. Delicious scents wafted off the snack table, and music filled the air.

I stood by one snack table now, glancing at the bridge leading to the mainland every few seconds in between watching Whisper greet her other friends and accept gifts. Her smile never faltered, but even she was hyper-focused on the bridge in anticipation of her moth prince's arrival.

"He better come," she said once she had fulfilled her duty as hostess and conceded to stand beside me. Leaning over the snack table, she snatched a cracker and popped it in her mouth.

"I'm sure the dear babysitter is just settling his charge into bed and will be here shortly."

Her eyes went wide. "Of course, *Adam* will be here. He wouldn't pass up all of this for anything." She twirled, her short, silk dress lifting teasingly higher as the gauzy layers caught the wind. "I mean to say *your* boy better come. Or I, without any trace of knowledge about him, will hunt him down and deliver his entrails to his parents on a silver platter."

Did Bay have parents? It hadn't really come up. Maybe we were both orphans? My cheeks heated at that thought, and shame made me look away from Whisper. I shouldn't hope for anyone to have lived with the same fears and complications of having been unwanted.

"What's the matter, chickie?" Whisper's concerned face poked in front of mine. Her delicate brows drew above pinched lips. "If he's not here shortly, he's unworthy. That simple." She glanced at the bridge again and huffed, folding her arms. "That will, indeed, go for both of us."

"It doesn't matter if he comes or not." The words felt heavy in my mouth. "It doesn't." Come the tenth of the month, he'd be gone, and I knew I had no right to think of it like abandonment, but he would be leaving me behind, and it was hard to see it in any other way.

A few more vibrantly dressed partygoers crossed the bridge, and Whisper sighed, fluffing her blond curls. "Pardon me, dearest. I'm afraid my subjects require my attention." Without another moment's notice, she darted through the center of the grove where people talked, swaying to the band, and pounced, hugging those who had just arrived.

Elaborate motions accompanied her conversation, and my stomach rocked, reminding me of Bay's vivid recollections just the night before. I wasn't like that. Them. Insecurity kept me wrapped in a thread that threatened to break at any moment. Doubts and fears clouded my head, suggesting I wasn't good enough or I wouldn't be. It was only a matter of time before everyone I held onto disappeared.

Maybe it would be best if he didn't come. If I didn't grow attached to someone else, someone I knew was scheduled to leave me.

"What's wrong, Wind Song?" The quiet, deep voice yanked me from every negative thought, and I whirled, facing Bay. He smiled, his skin absent of dust save the very top of his head, where some glittered, already fading.

"You came." I stared.

"I said I would."

"Yes, but…" Flushed, I dropped my gaze to our feet. I was worried he had been polite and hadn't wanted to waste any more time on me.

He curled a finger beneath my chin, bumping my attention back up to his face. "Dusk isn't a particularly precise time. If I'm late, that's my excuse."

A smile pulled on my lips. "Well? What do you think? I helped set up."

He gave the party a once-over that consisted of a half-second scrutiny before skimming his eyes over me for far longer. Clinging where my dress did, his gaze sampled and tasted and teased, then flicked away. He shoved his hands in his pockets, looking up at the sky. "It's very nice." His smile eased into a smirk. "The green compliments your hair."

I forced myself to hold onto dignity even though my hair wasn't the only thing that was red right now. "I never took you for a flirt."

"Really?" He shifted his stance. "You're either oblivious, or I'm bad at it then."

"Must be difficult to see underneath the assiness."

"Under the sassiness? I suppose so. It is my primary characteristic, the sass. Hard to see anything else beyond it, really."

I laughed, elbowing him, not for the first time. Keeping his hands in his pockets, he returned the shove awkwardly. A beat passed where he cleared his throat, and I gasped. "Could you be nervous?"

"What?"

"You're nervous, aren't you?"

His look turned incredulous, saying without so many words, "How dare you suggest such a thing, madam?" but his body language confirmed my suspicions.

"You're tense," I added.

He ruffled his hair, fingers catching in his braid and pulling it loose. Releasing a breath, he confessed, "You've found me out. I don't normally do things like this. Rather, I've *never* done something like this before."

"You've never gone to a party before?" With how frequent parties were on Skyla, I was justifiably shocked.

"I've never gone to a party with a girl before."

And now I was justifiably flattered. And he was considerably darker in the cheeks. My grin spread. "How old are you?"

"I'm…really not sure."

I looked him over from his brown hair down his muscular frame to his bare feet. "You look twenty. You act ten."

"Has anyone ever told you that you have a way with words, specifically to destroy self-esteem?"

"I don't believe it's come up, no."

We exchanged smiles, and I fought against the twinge of pain in my chest. After he left, when would he visit again? If he traveled the world, there was so much more to do out there than worry about seeing Skyla, or me.

Before I could gather enough courage to ask about his plans, a shrill gasp pulled both our attentions to Whisper. A hand before her mouth, she didn't bother concealing the way her eyes danced up and down, and up and down over Bay. "Oh. My. Yes." She blindly reached for my arm, touching my shoulder. "Yes." Brightening, she stepped forward, palm outstretched. "It's so nice to meet you. My name's Whispering Meadow, and I'm Lyric's best, dare I say, only friend."

Bay took her fingers, pressing a kiss to her knuckles, and I thought she would die right there. "Charmed to meet you. I'm just Bay."

I held myself back from a laugh.

"*Bay*. That's such a perfectly romantic name." Whisper sighed, her eyes going dreamy. As though she'd just remembered, she tossed a glance toward the bridge, then harrumphed. Spite edged her melodic voice when she mumbled, "How kind of you to be on time."

"So, I *was* on time." Bay's eyes stuck on me, his smile impish. "Lyric made me feel as though I was late. Maybe she was just overly anticipating my arrival."

"Was she now?" Whisper's voice pitched. Her lashes fluttered, the look in her eyes nothing short of manic. "How absolutely thrilling."

I glared at them both, attempting to stab them with my eyes. They hardly noticed.

"Well, if it doesn't work out between you two…I may just be available." She winked, and my heart stopped at the implication.

"I'm afraid I only go for redheads." Bay shrugged a shoulder, appearing casual, but some tension had filtered back into his body, and he pocketed his hands again.

I chewed my cheek, hoping Whisper would catch on. "We're not really…"

When my voice fizzled out, Bay interjected, "At least, not yet, anyway."

My eyes widened, and I wasn't sure if all the breath had escaped my chest or if I was holding it hostage.

He added, "Anything could happen." Dipping toward my ear, he whispered, "Unless, of course, you only consider me a ten-year-old."

Whisper cupped her hands over her mouth when Bay straightened, innocently watching dark clouds slip by the moon. Breathlessly, she said, "I like this. I like this a lot. You're perfect." She clasped his arm, forcefully prying his hand from his pocket so she could hold it. "Get married to my bestie and have a dozen sass-castic babies. I need them in my life."

He snickered. "Are you up for a dozen, Wind Song?"

"I think I should leave now." My heart was pounding. Despite him taking everything as calmly as anyone could, their teasing hit too close to hope for me. I liked the idea of him sticking around and making something more out of this, but that wasn't what he had planned, and I certainly wasn't going to bend any of his plans in a matter of days.

"'Wind Song'?" Whisper's grin rounded her cheeks. "We already have pet names? Can I just say I'm in love with both of you?"

To avoid her burning gaze, I glanced across the grove and released a pent-up breath; salvation had come to me at last. "Is that Adam?"

All joking died when Whisper whirled, spotting the dark-haired boy across the way. "How's my hair? Is my dress wrinkled, like, anywhere?" She stretched out her fingers, examining her nails, then shot me a pleading expression. "Am I wearing too much makeup?"

My eyes rolled. "You're a queen, Whisper. Go snag your prince."

She looked at Bay. "Male perspective?"

"If he likes you, it won't be because of how you look, but, no, you're not too shabby."

Whisper glowed. Snatching my pinky in hers, she pressed her forehead to mine, then said, "Keep him." In the next instant, she and her frothy dress were off like a streak.

I sighed, relaxing up until the moment I remembered I had to deal with the aftermath of her conversation with Bay. Peeking at him, I caught a lazy smirk and knew there would be no escaping. I had to ride out the waves she had caused.

"She's…something else." He passed me, perusing the snack table. "I can see why she's your best—pardon—only friend." Plucking a mini tart off a plate, he stuck it inside his vest.

Ignoring his words completely, I asked, "Skye came with you?"

"Of course. He's my best—pardon—only friend."

"And you're hiding him." That wasn't a question. "You knew it wasn't normal to talk with a pixie even though you acted like it was a few days ago."

"Or I could not have known until your reaction and be playing off it now so I don't stand out."

"I find that unlikely."

He popped another tart into his own mouth and twisted toward me on his heel. "Well, I can't control your thoughts, so have fun with them." He nodded toward the tree line behind me. "Let's sit over there where it's a bit more private."

I looked at the outskirts of the party where pixie floss threaded every tree, and dangling lanterns illuminated every shadow surrounding it. Before I replied, Bay strode past me and reclined against one of the oaks, relaxing for the first time since he'd arrived.

Skye snuck out of his pocket, joining the other pixies in the canopy, and Bay watched them, half a smile on his face.

Even without pixie dust covering every inch of his skin, he glowed, at one with the illuminated forest scene. When he patted the ground beside him, a piece of my heart lightened. I nearly glided to him and may have flown had any dust been on my skin. Sitting beside him, my back against the rough bark, I wondered if I fit just as perfectly in the picture or if I marred it. Attempting to relax as well as he had, I pulled off my satchel and set it beside me.

"You look very nice." His soft words barely reached

above the music, but after them, everything except his presence muffled, dropping away.

"So do you." I pushed my hair over my ear. "Did you take a bath or something?"

"Did I smell that bad before?"

My head whipped toward him. "I didn't mean—"

His playful grin stopped my words. "I know. Now look who's tense."

Folding my hands in my lap, I fooled with the simple green dress I wore. "Maybe we're both ten-year-olds."

He leaned close, his voice little more than a secretive purr. "You mean to say you've never been to a party with a boy before either?"

I mimicked the same secretive tone. "Nope." Setting the teasing aside, I sighed. Starlight bathed us, every twinkling light familiar and new all at once. "I spend most of my time exploring the islands, looking for adventures, but none ever come up. At least, not until meeting you."

"I'm an adventure, then?" He chuckled.

In complete seriousness, I murmured, "I think so. But I'm worried I won't get to be a part of it."

Tentative silence burdened with laughter and music and voices filled the space between us, keeping us so far from each other.

"Why can't you leave?"

I swallowed. Saying I wasn't allowed to felt so childish, and I didn't want to appear childish to him. The only real, logical attachment I had to him was the fact that he lived the life I longed for. Still, I wanted, needed, his approval. "I'm duty-bound to Skyla," I said instead. "I'm protecting it. Somehow."

Bay's brows knitted, but he didn't press the issue. Pulling a leg up to his chest, he rested an elbow on it and rubbed his lips with his thumb. "It's exhausting, what we do because of duty."

"Yeah…" My eyes drifted up, finding Whisper among everyone, and a laugh escaped me. "Well, I suppose they live happily ever after."

At the other side of the island, right on the edge where any wrong move would mean plummeting into the ocean, Whisper and Adam stood locked together. Her foot kicked up behind her, his lips on hers, their hands in one another's hair. Even from so far away, nothing but bliss shone off them. I smiled, anticipating all the details after the lights had gone out, and the party had slipped into silence.

My heart tripped, my gaze dropping to my hand. Beside it, just brushing, was Bay's. He continued staring ahead like he hadn't moved closer, but his quirked lips gave him away entirely. Mischief and innocence radiated in his expression.

I told myself not to take it seriously and wracked my brain for another topic, something to say. "Are you really leaving in two days?" The second the words left me, my eyes closed, and I bit my tongue.

"I am." His hand didn't move. His gaze didn't redirect. Only sorrow tinted his smile, and I knew somewhere deep within me. I had nothing to do with it.

"Will you be back?" I confined myself to the shameful questions, deciding if I'd started down this path, I may as well not back out.

"I always come back. But I never know when." Now, he looked at me, and we were far closer than we'd been before. I could pick out golden flecks dancing in his hazel eyes. They were soft, and maybe it was a trick of the light, but they were beautiful. His lips parted to say something, but a shriek sliced through me.

My heart stopped cold. A wash of ice chilled me to the bone.

I'd know that voice anywhere.

Jumping to my feet, I zoned in on Whisper in the moment after a man crashed into her, sending them both over the edge toward an unforgiving sea.

From this height, she would die.

She would die.

She would die.

My legs moved on their own, force slamming through my joints. Sheer terror closed my throat, blocking all my breath. I couldn't see anything but the panic in her eyes as she'd fallen. I couldn't hear anything but her shriek, on replay. I plowed through everyone, caring less if they all fell than if she did.

Without thought or pause, I dove after her.

Wind whipped my hair, her dress. The man who had pushed her was nowhere in sight. She kept her body flat to the wind, slowing her descent, but not enough.

"Lyric!" she screamed. Her eyes searched me, and I realized moments after her brown skin went ashy that I didn't have my satchel; I didn't have any dust.

"It's okay!" I yelled, knowing it wasn't, but hoping it might be. I had fallen countless times before. I trusted the pixies would catch me—if they knew, if they made it in time. Air burned my eyes, tears dashed away before they could roll down my cheeks. "We will never be apart." I caught up to her, touching her hand. She gripped my fingers, her tears slapping against my face.

Her smile shook as we both stretched our bodies to give us as much time as we could garner. Near my ear, nearly lost to the roaring wind, she murmured, "I wish we were apart now, Lyly. I'm so sorry."

I held her. The churning waters below were dark and formless, depthless, a pool of ink streaming closer with every lost moment. Everything in my head was a blur. I had never been afraid of falling; I had always been afraid of losing my best—and only—friend.

Now, I may not need to be afraid of either ever again.

Closing my eyes, I embraced whatever fate held.

"Fly, you idiot!" Bay's voice screamed, and Whisper was wrenched from my arms. A hand gripped my clothes, yanking my body up. *"Fly!"*

A glimmer of dust surrounded me, and I screeched to a stop, suspended in the air. My heart panicked, jerked from accepting death to understanding it wouldn't come today. I looked at Bay, who held Whisper over his shoulder and searched the water. "There," he said, darting for a dark spot.

I looked at Skye, who chirped and beckoned me after. I followed Bay to an outcropping of an island and rushed to Whisper's side when he dumped her in the sand. "Hey!" I growled. "Be careful!"

"Yes, you're welcome." His face was hard as stone, no care in his expression. He scanned the waves, his lip curled, then he lifted off the ground and zipped into the dark.

Whisper held a hand at her head, blinking after Bay and Skye. "He…has a pixie with him?"

"Are you okay?" I clasped her hand, unable to care less what Bay was up to.

Her lashes fluttered, and a waterfall of tears streamed down her cheeks. Her chest rose and fell in horrid, uneven motions, and her beautiful, dainty face contorted. "N-no. We almost died. W-what… W-who…" She was such an ugly crier, always feeling every emotion completely. "I want my moth prince," she blubbered.

My heart still thudded irregularly, but we were okay. We were okay. I had to remember that if I was going to keep my sanity. Dropping my forehead to hers, I took deep breaths and forced myself to get a grip. Who had shoved her and jumped off the edge themselves? And why?

"No trace." Bay interrupted my thoughts, and I looked up. He emerged from the water, shaking out his hair. Waves crashed behind him, and Skye circled his head, dousing him anew in dust before sitting on his shoulder. "Did you see him clearly at all, Whispering Meadow?"

She sniffled. "What?"

"The man. Did you see at all what he looked like?"

Whisper's head began to shake, her lip quivering, but she stopped. "There was a flash of light, and he was gone. But the light reflected on something gold for a split second. Maybe an earring?"

Bay's jaw clenched. "Was it large and hooped?"

Dumbly, Whisper nodded.

"Pirate," Bay growled, cramming his fingers into his

hair. His braid came loose, and Skye caught the tie before the lapping tide could snatch it away. Pacing, Bay inhaled and exhaled deeply; then he stopped. "Okay. You both need to get back home. I don't think you can fly, but we can both manage to carry you." He pointed at Whisper, and my eyes widened.

"Of course, she—"

"I can't."

My heart stopped again. "What?"

Shame tainted her tear-streaked cheeks, her wobbly smile pleading. "I'm sorry, Lyly… I haven't been able to since…since Papa left. I don't like to think about it, and I didn't know how to tell you."

"But we were—" My words came out breathless before I cut them short and swallowed. That was a topic for later. We needed to get home safe and figure out why there had been two pirates in Skyla. Peter had to believe me if all three of us told him. We needed to do something about it before anything else like this happened, or worse.

After all, why were they here? Surely, they weren't visiting to pay their respects to a boy who had killed their kind for sport.

"How do you have a pixie?" Whisper asked, slowly gaining her feet. I helped support her, and after she was stable, she released my hand.

"Doesn't everyone?" Bay brushed her surprise aside, squinting upward. At Skyla.

It hit me then, shoving everything else from my brain.

I wasn't on Skyla. I was in the real world. For the first time in my life, my feet rested on grounded earth. I stood in front of the ocean I always saw from so far above. It rolled, each wave a distinct creature, and I couldn't find words.

"Wind Song, are you still with us?" Bay's voice was more gentle than it had been for the past few minutes.

I focused on him, nodding.

He glanced out at the waves, a hint of a smile lifting his lips. It was small, but it proved no matter how many times he had seen it, he'd never lost the wonder. "It is beautiful." Clapping his hands together, he jerked us from the moment. "Okay, Skye, do your thing."

The pixie dropped Bay's hair tie into his hand and spun over Whisper and I. Even if she couldn't use the magic to fly herself, with our support, being doused in it would make carrying her back up easier.

We each took a side and lifted her through the air to the deserted party location. Lanterns still swayed in the wind, and pixies still darted through the trees, oblivious. But, the piles of food had been abandoned, save for the stray pixie who had decided they belonged to it now.

"Whisper…" The soft voice made my friend tense, and her head whipped up the second her feet touched the ground. Her brown eyes widened, and she yanked her arms free from around our shoulders to scrub her face. Thankfully she hadn't been wearing too much makeup, but it still was clear in her puffy eyes that she had been fiercely crying.

"Adam, what are you—"

The large boy wrapped her in a hug before she could get her sentence out. Bay and I spared one another a glance when Adam's lip quivered. He bit it, sucking in a breath. "After Lyric jumped, I thought you'd have to be all right."

Whisper laughed shortly, still shaken. "Naturally."

Adam's eyes snapped open on Bay and me, settling on Bay. "But why did you…"

"Faith and trust," Bay mumbled, passing by them, "'Lyly' was missing one last thing, so I brought it to her." He headed for the trees where my satchel lay, useless. I would never take it off again.

Whisper pulled out of Adam's hold and shook her head. "It doesn't matter. What does matter is I'm okay, and you're okay, and everyone is okay. We need to get home now. Only Lyric knows how to get to Peter at this time, and he needs to know what happened immediately."

Adam's brows furrowed. He glanced at me before rustling his dark hair and addressing Whisper. "Yeah …, okay. May I walk you home?"

Flushing, Whisper looked at me, her wide smile almost erasing the faint streaks smudged over her cheeks. "Are you okay?"

I extended my pinky. "Of course."

"Even with…" She pressed her lips together and linked her finger with mine. When she leaned forward to press our foreheads together, she whispered, "I'm sorry. I meant to tell you, but I couldn't."

I watched her and Adam walk away, ignoring the empty feeling spinning in my chest. Too much was changing at once. If Whisper couldn't fly, our plans of leaving together and seeing the world evaporated. Even though she had said if it came to a choice between Adam and me she'd choose me, I wouldn't want to take her from the happily ever after she had been searching for since we were kids.

My throat tightened. We said we'd never be apart, and now, I knew if ever we were, it would be because I had broken the oath. I would be the one who abandoned her.

Bay dangled my satchel before my face, blocking the view of the bridge where I remained staring despite Whisper and Adam having vanished several minutes ago. He dropped the bag into my hands before elaborating a bow. "May *I* have the pleasure of walking you home?"

I slipped the strap over my head, adjusting the bag at my waist where pixie dust would never be far from my hands again. Then I looked at him. "Nope."

His brow quirked as he straightened. "Why not?"

"My house is like your house, secret. But unlike yours, mine is well-hidden."

"Ouch. After I saved your life too." He glanced over his shoulder where his pixie perused the snack tables with several other of his kind. "I suppose the party is left to the wild things now."

The melody of the night and the chirring of pixies surrounded us. "I guess so."

He rebraided his hair, sighing. "May I walk you back to the mainland, at least?" When his braid was tied, his gaze averted. "And will I see you tomorrow?"

I looked at my moccasins, wanting to say yes.

"I'm not leaving without saying goodbye, even if I have to hunt down your secret house before I go."

I rolled my eyes. "I guess I have no choice, then."

"Not really, no." His smile drifted away, and he

looked at the edge of the island. "Skye," he said into the wind, but the pixie heard him, "let's go."

Our walk was silent as we headed through Aire, both our heads seemingly packed with thoughts. I couldn't tell why seeing the pirate had rattled him so much unless, of course, his talk about knowing blades and not pirates was a lie. Who knew where his adventures had taken him. I still didn't know what country the map above his bed belonged to. I had studied it that night a few days ago, and the image wouldn't soon leave my head. Nothing from these brief days would.

Stopping when we reached the trees on my home island, I toyed with my satchel's flap. "This is my stop."

Bay peered around the area, scouring the treetops for any hint of construction. He'd find nothing of the sort. Huffing, he crossed his arms and examined me as though I'd give away the secret.

I smiled pleasantly and batted my eyelashes.

A sliver of moonlight cascaded through the treetops, catching his eye, and the gleam that followed made my chest tighten and my heart skip a beat. His hand raised, my gaze darting to it, and even in the dim light, I could tell hard work had calloused his fingers. He moved close, catching a flaming lock between his fingers and tucking it behind my ear. The barest touch of his skin sent a shiver careening through me, and… I didn't want to say goodbye. Not tonight. Not tomorrow.

Before my mouth could open and I could beg for something I'd regret, Peter's voice shredded the forest. "LYRIC!"

I jerked back, away from Bay, and faced the boy speeding through the trees. Tinkerbell glared at his side, per usual. Alight with dust in the moonlight, he appeared little more than a will o' the wisp.

"You're okay," he panted, ignoring Bay entirely as he clapped his hands against my cheeks and turned my head this way and that. "You're okay?"

"I'm fine." I swatted him off me. "How'd you hear about what happened?"

"Apparently, Tiger Lily knows where we live." He grumbled; his brows furrowed. "I had no idea."

I'd suspected as much, even though she'd never said anything. Tiger Lily raised me on stories of her and Peter's adventures, stories Peter had long forgotten when she'd aged.

"Some people went to her house and said there had been an accident, and you were involved."

Likely Whisper's other guests had gone straight to her mother. I swallowed. "Did Tiger Lily tell you exactly what had happened?"

"Only that you and I guess one of your friends had fallen." His furrowed brows made me wonder if he'd forgotten the more important detail that someone had shoved 'one of my friends' over the edge before disappearing without a trace.

My mouth opened, but Bay beat me to words. "You never mentioned you had a little brother, Wind Song."

I blinked. Peter blinked. Tinkerbell blinked, turning in Peter's hair to face Bay. Her head tilted so far, she nearly went upside down.

Peter didn't grace him with a glance. "I'm her father. Now, what exactly happened, Lyric?"

"Her *father*?" Concern rippled over Bay's face.

Peter whirled then, floating off the ground to meet

Bay's height. "Yes. Who in Skyla are you? What are you doing here?"

Bay's lips parted and closed several times, his eyes flicking between me and my underage parental unit before he managed, "I'm a friend. From the party. I wanted to make sure she got home safe."

Peter scoffed, folding his arms. Long moments passed, and his lips pursed. "She hasn't mentioned you before. It's always a girl. I know it's always a girl." He looked over his shoulder at me, and I held my breath. Snapping his fingers, he stated, "Tiger Lily's girl. Yeah. It's always Tiger Lily's girl. You're not Tiger Lily's girl."

"No...sir...I'm not."

If the moment weren't entirely insane, I might have laughed at how, well, insane it was.

Bay's gaze narrowed. "You're Peter Pan, then."

Peter stuck his nose in the air. "Who else would I be?"

"How old are you?" Bay's eyes were intent on Peter, and his body retained a stillness that sent chills down my spine. *What did it matter how old Peter was?*

"Why would you expect me to know? I'm older than her and older than you and older than Skyla itself. I obviously have more important things to think about."

"Obviously," Bay murmured, and the dark glint in his eye made me stiffen. When he looked at me, the feeling was gone. "I suppose I'll leave you in your father's capable hands."

"Right."

He raised a hand, turned around, and walked away. When he had disappeared in the foliage, Peter remained glaring after him. "He had dust." The intensity in his voice disappeared when he faced me again. "You have dust."

Tinkerbell chimed, and Peter harrumphed.

"She recognizes who it belongs to, but says I won't remember."

My stomach flipped, but I shoved the comment aside, knowing Peter was nothing if not easy to distract. "It doesn't matter. It's the only reason I'm alive right now. But, Peter, I know you didn't believe me before about the pirate, but Whisper, my friend, Tiger Lily's girl, didn't just fall off the island. Another pirate pushed her, then he disappeared midair."

Peter remained silent, and anger built behind my eyes. He didn't believe me *again*. Skyla was probably under attack, and yet, he didn't believe me. Rubbing his nose, he dropped his gaze. "No, the boys and I…we looked after you told us. Felt bad for making you cry and all… I believe you. But this is very bad." His fists clenched. "We'll figure it out. What have I always told you? We'll figure it out; Peter Pan always does." Determination burned in his eyes, and I knew this was only the beginning.

9TH NOVEMBER

"What?" I stared at Peter, baffled. I couldn't have just heard what I thought I'd heard.

"Stay put today."

Okay, maybe I did. I planted my hands on my hips and glared down at him. "Excuse me. I'm not a child. You can't just ground me to my room because you think it might be dangerous outside."

"It *is* dangerous outside. You've come across two pirates in a single week. We don't know why they're here, but I have a hunch it might have something to do with you. This is the most secure place in Skyla, so *stay put.*"

I threw my hands in the air. "Why would it have anything to do with me? I'm inconsequential. I wasn't even born when you fought against the pirates."

Peter's eyes narrowed, searching for something. He clamped his hand against his mouth, then murmured, "Maybe. Maybe not. Just stay here for a day while I figure things out."

"Oh, and I can't help you figure things out?" No, that's not what I wanted to say. Shaking my head, I breathed. "Listen, you don't understand. I'm going to stay out of trouble. This is just the last day I'll get to see my friend before he moves away. I don't know when he'll visit again."

Peter sneered. "I don't trust that kid from last night. Good riddance to him."

Anger sparked. I stomped out of my room toward the exit. "Well, you can't keep me here."

Peter scratched the back of his head. "Chubs."

The hefty boy saluted and planted himself in the exit, blocking it completely. Stomping my foot, I exclaimed, "That's not fair!"

"It's for your own good." Peter actually looked exhausted when he rubbed his eyes. "Listen, I'm sorry this coincides with your friend leaving, but I'd be lost without you, Skyla'd be lost without you."

My heart pinched, and it hurt to swallow. "I'm not magical. I'm not special. I'm not some protective amulet that is keeping Skyla afloat, Peter. I'm just…me. An orphan who was abandoned in the clouds." Holding back my tears, I scanned his face. "But you'll never accept that because you always forget the important things."

"Lyric…I—"

Walking past him, I shut myself in my room, slipping to the floor beside my bed. My legs pulled tight against my chest, I refused to cry. In the past few days, I had cried too much. Nothing came from the tears, but plans boiled from the anger.

I was going to see Bay before he left. I was going to get to the bottom of this mystery.

And I was certain the boy and the mystery were shrouded as one.

I had two books, only two, and I kept them in my satchel along with some food, my telescope, the bag of pixie dust, a pair of gloves, and my pan flute. Though I'd read them countless times before, they were all I had now to pass the time between my argument with Peter and when Chubs inevitably fell asleep in front of the exit.

My ears perked when the soft snores drifted throughout the small home, and I tucked my novel back into my bag. Creeping to my door, I peeked out. Chubs sat in the exit, his face crammed against the wall. His mouth was open, and drool leaked onto his fur clothing. No one else was in view.

I scanned several times before gathering the courage to sprinkle some dust on my head and tiptoe toward him. At the exit, I listened past the snores to make sure no one was returning. When I was certain I could make it out unnoticed, I floated into the air above Chubs and out into the night.

Not wasting any time, I darted for Bay's island, landing on the porch. I brushed back my hair, raised my hand, and watched the door open before I could knock.

"There you are." Bay's gaze ran over me from head to toe. "I thought I'd have to hunt you down. Is everything okay?"

Within, his oil lamp flickered light over strewn

papers and curling maps. I recognized the landmarks peeking out as the same ones found on the map above his cot. "Where is that?" I asked, ignoring his question.

He turned, stilling. Running his hand over his hair, he shrugged. "Elsewhere."

"That's where you're going? Why?" I slipped past him and crouched, spreading the curling page flat.

"It's where I have to go." He floated to the ground across from me, catching my hand before I could completely view the next map flat. "Why do you have to be so nosy?"

I stared at him.

Bay's fingers left mine, clenching into a fist. "You aren't here for a casual visit and then a goodbye, are you?"

My head shook. Wordlessly, I dropped my gaze, peeled back the curled edge of the map, and saw the etched visage of a pirate ship. A bleeding red skull marked it. "You knew that pirate," I murmured. "Why are they here? Is it because you are?"

"No. I don't know why they're here." He paused, swallowed, and continued, "I do have a hunch."

Skye appeared out of nowhere, chiming madly at Bay. The little pixie's hands were splayed in objection, but Bay scrubbed a hand over his face. "I know. I know!" Torment darkened his eyes, but he made them meet mine. "She's been hidden away here all her life by Pan. And she might just be the only hope for both us and Skyla."

"What are you talking about?"

Bay kicked up a leg and rested his arm against it, cradling his forehead in his hand. "I know it's not normal to talk with pixies, certainly not at my age. I know most our age can't fly. We both know Pan, probably better than he remembers to know himself. We have a hunch about why the pirates are here, and we have encountered them…many, many times before. I don't know my age because I'm older than I look and younger than I feel."

"You aren't making any sense."

He laughed, but it was bitter. "No, I suppose I'm not."

"Just tell me plainly why I've seen two pirates in the past few days when I'd never seen any before."

"Two?" His jaw tightened.

Right, he hadn't been here then. "I saw one and chased him to the island where Peter keeps his pirate ship. I pinned him down, but before I could get any answers, he began foaming at the mouth…then he died."

"Appeared to." Bay cursed beneath his breath.

"No, he definitely did. Peter saw him afterward."

"Sure." Bay divided his attention between his thoughts and Skye, completely ignoring me, so I slammed my hand against the floor. He glanced up, and Skye's tinkling words stopped.

"Explain," I growled. "I came here for answers."

Bay lounged back. "And here I thought you enjoyed my company." When my expression didn't crack, he sighed. "Okay. I'm sorry. It's hard to explain the magic the pirates have come into. I learned a long time ago not to trust any of them if they 'died.' Pirates are selfish. They aren't as loyal to their captains as their captains would like to believe. If threatened, they will tell you everything. And they definitely aren't going to kill themselves to keep any secrets."

"So how did he..."

"Short answer? Magic. Long answer? Powerful magic. The kind pirates don't normally have, so I know they are getting help. From where or whom...that's something I haven't been able to solve."

My heart pounded, picking up in tempo. "Why are you fighting the pirates?"

"Fighting them?" He laughed. "I'm not. They simply keep getting in my way. And I think I won't tell you what I'm up to. At least not right now. Maybe if...you came with me, though..."

I froze, down to the blood in my veins. "W-what?"

"Come with me." His smile was carefree, gentle, enticing like we hadn't been talking about villains with powerful magic that were infesting my home. Skye chirped, looking at me too, waiting. When I still didn't respond, couldn't find the words, Bay tapped the map between us. "To elsewhere, to Neverland."

My lips parted, my eyes widening. I felt I'd heard that title before, in the corners of Peter's stories, though, he'd never mentioned it by name. Why? Why did something I'd never known existed feel so familiar?

Bay continued, "If your enemy is the pirates, why not meet them where they are? Shave them off bit by bit before they ever reach Skyla?"

"I can't." My own words surprised me. I wanted nothing more than to go with him, to Neverland, to this magical place that his stories lived and breathed in, but I couldn't. I couldn't leave Peter or Whisper, especially if we were under attack. I had to be here for them. Not because I was some lucky charm. If Whisper were at risk, I could throw a blade. I could fly. Not many on our island could both fight and use the magic of the pixies. "If they are already coming, we'll have to be ready for them. I'll have to fight for my home."

Maybe this was why I had been left here all those years ago.

Bay rubbed his jaw. "Okay. I get it." Skye settled on his shoulder while he scanned the map. "I don't know when I'll be back. Even if the pirates leave Neverland and you defeat them, it won't guarantee my success."

Those words weighed against my body, but I nodded, lifting the flap to my pack. "Then I guess we have tonight." Bringing out some bread, cheese, and berries, I offered him a weak smile.

He reached forward, moving his face close to mine when he grabbed one ripe, blackberry. "Don't you forget me."

My cheeks heated, but he moved back before he was close enough to feel his breath on my lips. I whispered, "Never."

We talked about silly things, stupid things, stories, fears, dreams. We talked like tomorrow we wouldn't say goodbye. We talked through the night, though I hadn't meant to stay so long. We talked curled together though I'd never meant to end up in his arms.

We talked.

We laughed.

And I, maybe a little bit, right before accidentally falling asleep, cried.

10TH NOVEMBER

Heavy thuds marred my dreams, shaking the foundation of my imagination. The pictures in my head distorted till they burned around the edges. The charred pieces closed in, then popped.

I jolted upright, gasping, and peered at the small room before me. Bay's house. Bay. I must have fallen asleep? Turning my head, I looked at him. He rubbed his face, meeting my eyes before noting our precarious sleeping position—me in his arms—with half a smirk.

I couldn't think on it for more than an instant. Dawn streamed through the windows. Gongs screamed in steady beats, metal clamoring to be heard across all of Skyla.

"What is that airwoman-forsaken noise?" Bay murmured his voice thick with rest.

The sleepy tenor may have made my cheeks go hot at any other point in time, but my body was awash in ice. "The warning signal."

"What?"

I scrambled to my feet, checked for my bag, and rushed to the door. "I have to go. I have to go now. This could be it. What if the pirates are here?"

Bay's eyes widened. Zipping off the floor and to his cot, he snatched Skye off the blanket and poked the little pixie's cheeks. Skye awoke complaining before he tilted his head to the noise.

"Dust her," he commanded, and Skye dashed into the air toward me without question. Bay added, "It's faster to fly than run."

Glitter ran over my skin, tingling as it fell, and my feet left the wooden planks. "Thank you. Are you coming?"

He shook his head. "If the pirates are here, they can't see me. I can't risk fighting them. I'm sorry…I…"

"I don't understand, but I do." Every loud hammering sound reminded me of all I had to lose, but I flew into Bay's arms, squeezing him tight for as long as I dared. "I'll miss you. Good luck."

Strong, large hands clamped against my back, fingers splayed, leaving a sensation I didn't think I'd ever be able to forget. He whispered, "Good luck to you too."

When I left, I didn't look back. Wind whipped against my cheeks, the warmth biting as I streaked toward the capital. I searched the air and the sea and the ground for any signs of danger. I saw nothing.

A sense of calm nearly took hold. Perhaps Peter had panicked when he checked my room and found me missing? I could find him, get yelled at, and everything would be okay. We would have more time to prepare, and then when the pirates did come, we would be ready.

Changing my focus, I looked for brilliant orange hair.

Instead, I found a crowd of people toward the far end of the mainland, standing just before the path to Whisper's neighborhood.

"No." My throat closed. My heartbeat grew short.

The bridge meant to connect the islands dangled like a broken wing, limp and frayed like it had snapped. The island itself rested in the water far below, cracked. Jagged stone and wood protruded across the surface of collapsed homes. Clumps of dirt drifted in heaps, bobbing with the waves.

Peter rose from the rubble, hovering in front of the crowd. Before he opened his mouth, I slammed into him, clutching his shoulders. His eyes went wide, relief filling them moments later. "You're okay. When we couldn't find you, I thought perhaps—"

"Where is she?" I demanded, clipping his words.

His brows knitted, and his head tilted.

"Where is she!"

"We don't know the damage yet. Bombs went off at the base of each tree some time ago. They woke everyone. The pixies helped whoever could fly, and those who could make it jumped into the ocean." He scratched his head, but I wasn't hearing anything reassuring. Whisper lived in the center of the island. She couldn't fly. He continued, "The boys are helping—"

I pushed him aside and fled toward the fractured land where I'd spent half my life, so much of my childhood. "Whisper!" I screamed. Tears blurred my vision. We had just survived near-death. We had just made it.

"No." I panted. Breath raked in and out of my lungs

as I sped from one broken section of land to the next. "Tiger Lily!" My voice broke. Lips trembling, I hugged myself, whirling and blinking fast. I couldn't miss her because I was crying; I had to clear my eyes. She was fine. She just needed help. I had to find her and help her.

"WHISPER!" I caught sight of her house. The roof was tilted, the walls caved in, and I imagined her trapped inside, bleeding, cold. I couldn't stomach the images that followed, so I dashed forward, scraping my knees when I fell to them on the rough ground. I clawed my way to an opening and peered in through the shadows.

Her perfect new dress lay tattered, halfway beneath a fallen beam and covered in a thick, red liquid. Nothing moved. Waves and people and noise and the incessant gongs filled my ears till my head boiled, but all was silent.

"You said you wouldn't leave me!" I screamed into the hole. "You promised! Every day!"

"Lyric!" Peter pulled me away from the house, turning my head to face him. I couldn't see anything. I couldn't feel anything. I couldn't hear anything. Images of her suffering and trapped and drowning and alone crammed their way into my skull until I was right there with her, suffocating in a dozen different ways.

"Lyric, breathe!" Peter yelled.

And I was. I was breathing. But I was breathing too much, and there was no air.

"Lyric, damn it." I'd never heard him curse before. "C'mon. You're okay. Twins! Get the others! Help me with her. Let's get her somewhere safer." He wrapped his arms around me, and I faintly registered Tinkerbell chiming soothing tones in my ear just before it all went dark.

Whisper smiled at me, but something wasn't right. She wasn't completely clear. Something muffled her laugh, and it was gone too soon. Everything around me got darker and darker, then I could hear other voices.

"We've searched everywhere, Peter." Tootles.

"We've lost a group of people." One twin.

And the other: "Including Tiger Lily…"

There was a pause while I pried my eyes open. Something thick wanted to keep them closed, so I rubbed away a gooey crust and squinted into the dim space.

"Who's Tiger Lily?"

Instantly awake, I jerked upright. Peter stood in the center of our home with his arms folded, each Lost Boy before him. Genuine confusion muddled his expression, and the boys looked at one another.

Slightly saw me first, extending a finger. "Ay, she's up."

That set aside the conversation—for them.

"*Who's Tiger Lily*?" My voice cracked, raw from something—screaming? "What are you talking about?"

Peter stared at me. "Was she a friend of yours?"

I stumbled out of Peter's large chair, dropping the blankets they had covered me with. Focusing on each Lost Boy, I asked, "Did you find Whisper? Is Tiger Lily…really…?"

Sadness pulled their expressions down, then one at a

time they murmured, "Tiger Lily? What did she look like?"

"A friend of yours?"

"Everyone is gathered on the mainland. You could go look?"

Their eyes betrayed them, sorrow gleaming in their averted gazes. But when I turned toward Peter, I found nothing of the sort. His brows were lowered with concern, but nothing more.

"Are you okay, Lyric?"

My head shook, and my lips parted dumbly. "It happens that quickly?" I trembled, taking a step back when he took one closer. "How long has it been? A few hours?"

"It's nearly dusk," one Lost Boy offered; I wasn't sure whom. Sound distorted in my head, blurring until I heard the phantom of Whisper's laugh, something I would never hear again.

"What's gotten into you?" Peter rubbed the back of his neck. "We have to make a plan to strike against the pirates who did this."

The pirates who did this. Of course. That's why they had been here. To thin our numbers before their attack. My fists clenched, anger overwhelming the empty feeling residing in my gut. Nails biting flesh, I turned around.

"Lyric?" True bafflement coated Peter's voice. "Where are you going?"

"To check and see if my friend's among the survivors." I knew she wasn't.

"Be back soon so we can plan."

I ignored his words as I climbed outside and opened

my satchel. Lifting my pouch of pixie dust, I sprinkled just enough to take me to Bay's house on my head. I would scour his maps and notes until I found my way to Neverland, to the pirates who had done this, then I would make them pay.

My throat closed as I soared through the early night, sped along by a rush of wind. Light hues blanketed the sky still, but two or three stars blinked on in the twilight. I rubbed my eyes. Tears were getting me nowhere. And yet I couldn't make them stop.

I landed directly on Bay's porch, sniffling, and reached for the door. I had to pull myself together, let anger guide my steps, or I wouldn't have what it took to fight when I found the pirates responsible. But I couldn't shake the urge to scream. How could she be gone? After all we'd been through, I couldn't picture my life without her nearby.

"Wind Song?" Bay's voice drifted through the night, starkly soft compared to the screaming in my head.

I looked behind me, down at him. His eyes widened where he stood on the grass. Moments later, he was hovering in front of me, just beyond the porch rail.

"What…happened?"

"You haven't left yet?" I croaked. He shook his head. I didn't have words. I couldn't find anything to say clearly. "The pirates, they… She's gone, and I…" *I did nothing*. Couldn't do anything. What if I had been there? If I had just been there. A sob caught in my chest as I tunneled my fingers into my hair and gripped the ends until my scalp stung.

"Hey." Bay touched my hand, trying to pull it free.

He gave up, awkwardly drawing me toward his chest. "It's okay. Are the pirates still here?"

It wasn't okay! Nothing was okay! I wanted to scream and hit him, but instead, all I could manage was a limp, "No."

"Who's gone?"

My jaw tightened until my teeth ached, but I captured a single breath. "Whisper."

Bay stilled.

Everything unleashed then in a tide. The bombs. The island falling. Tiger Lily and Whisper. How Peter had forgotten in less than a day. How I felt empty and lost and scared. I had to be strong, but I couldn't stop shaking.

She had abandoned me.

I couldn't be sure how long I cried, but it was well over an hour. The night was full by the time I ambled to Bay's side again. He sat on the porch, gazing up at the heavens, having allowed me to mourn in his house for as long as I needed.

"I hope you didn't get snot all over everything in there." He offered me half a smile, but I couldn't return the expression even for his sake.

My skin felt clammy, and everything was numb right down to my toes. How had so much changed in so short a time? Just last week, I was wandering the woods in my usual routine, thinking about exploring the world beyond, thinking about Whisper's birthday party, dreaming about the adventures we would have. Then, we both nearly died. And I found out she couldn't fly. And now she was really gone.

Maybe Peter had been right all along. Maybe I was lucky, but in the same way, he was. No matter what came our way, we continued even when others didn't have that luxury.

"It's nearly time," Bay murmured into my thoughts.

I looked at him. "What do you mean?"

He pointed up through the branches at two gleaming stars. "Do you see the second star on the right?" I did. "That's where we need to fly. To reach Neverland."

I stared at it. "So, Star Boy really came directly from a star." My voice was absent of emotion, but he didn't mind.

"Yup." A tentative pause passed between us where I could feel his eyes on me, looking deeper than I dared to right now. "Are you sure you—"

"Yes." There was no doubt about that—none at all in my mind. If I left, I could avenge Whisper. If I died trying, the only person I left behind now would forget about me in a matter of hours. Maybe if he didn't know I was dead, he'd remember me for a few days.

Maybe the second I disappeared into that dark sky, he'd ask: *Lyric, who?*

That thought soured my tongue, nearly bringing back an onslaught of tears, but there were none left. "I have to go. I don't have anything left to lose, and there's no one really left to lose me."

Bay laughed, standing, and my brows furrowed. He extended a hand to me, Skye just over his shoulder, waiting and watching. "Well, that's not true. I'm still here. And I'll be damned if I lose you. Understood?"

The ghost of what may have been a smile a few days ago lifted my lips as I clasped his hand. Warmth sparked through his fingers, a residue of dust allowing me to float off the porch with him. "I understand," I replied before Skye doused me in dust and hugged my cheek for the barest moment. It was enough to bolster my courage and make me grip Bay's hand tighter.

"Take me to Neverland, Star Boy."

He faced the twinkling sky, the specks of light reflecting in his hazel eyes. His chest filled with breath, determination etched in his expression. His lips barely moved, but I heard him, crystal clear: "Away we go."

And away we went.

Continue the story in Heiress of Stars

A NOTE FROM THE AUTHOR

The Kingdom of Fairytales authors hope you enjoyed this new way of reading. We don't think that a series has ever been set with one chapter a day thought a whole year before and we hope we did it justice.

With this in mind, please leave a review, but when you do, remember that these books were always meant to be short breaks in your day and the blurb reflects that.

We would LOVE it if you can drop us a few words on Amazon

Review here

AFTER THE HAPPILY EVER AFTER…

There is more to these stories. You want to know what happens next right? Fast forward eighteen years…

Pick up book one now

PREQUEL

SLEEPING BEAUTY

1. Queen of Dragons
2. Heiress of Embers
3. Throne of Fury
4. Goddess of Flames

LITTLE MERMAID

5. Queen of Mermaids
6. Heiress of the Sea
7. Throne of Change
8. Goddess of Water

RED RIDING HOOD

9. King of Wolves
10. Heir of the Curse
11. Throne of Night
12. God of Shifters

RAPUNZEL

13. King of Devotion
14. Heir of Thorns
15. Throne of Enchantment
16. God of Loyalty

RUMPELSTILTSKIN

17. Queen of Unicorns
18. Heiress of Gold
19. Throne of Sacrifice
20. Goddess of Loss

BEAUTY AND THE BEAST

21. King of Beasts
22. Heir of Beauty
23. Throne of Betrayal
24. God of Illusion

ALADDIN

25. Queen of the Sun
26. Heiress of Shadows
27. Throne of the Phoenix
28. Goddess of Fire

CINDERELLA

29. Queen of Song
30. Heiress of Melody

31. Throne of Symphony
32. Goddess of Harmony

ALICE IN WONDERLAND

33. Queen of Clockwork
34. Heiress of Delusion
35. Throne of Cards
36. Goddess of Hearts

WIZARD OF OZ

37. King of Traitors
38. Heir of Fugitives
39. Throne of Emeralds
40. God of Storms

SNOW WHITE

41. Queen of Reflections
42. Heiress of Mirrors
43. Throne of Wands
44. Goddess of Magic

PETER PAN

45. Queen of Skies
46. Heiress of Stars
47. Throne of Feathers
48. Goddess of Air

URBIS

49. Kingdom of Royalty
50. Kingdom of Power
51. Kingdom of Fairytales
52. Kingdom of Ever After

JOIN US

Would you like to get Bay's adventure logs? Click the link below to pick your free gift up.

Kingdom of Fairytales FREE gift

Check the Kingdom of Fairytales website for competitions, news and info on all the books and authors

Kingdom of Fairytales Website

Or Join us on our Kingdom of Fairytales Facebook page for fun, games and author takeovers

Still want more? Completely immerse yourself in the Kingdom of Fairytales experience and pick up exclusive offers and gifts

Become a Patron

THE KINGDOM OF FAIRYTALES TEAM

These books would not be written without a great many people. Here is our team:

Many thanks to those who have made this possible.

Thank you to Rhi Parkes without whom, this series would never have come about.

Thanks to all the authors.

J.A. Armitage, Audrey Rich, B. Kristen Mcmichael, Emma Savant, Jennifer Ellision, Scarlett Kol, R. Castro, Margo Ryerkerk, Zara Quentin, Laura Greenwood and Anne Stryker

Also thank you to our amazing Beta team

Nadine Peterse-Vrijhof, Diane Major, Kalli Bunch and Stephanie Pittser.

Thanks to our Proof Reader

Tina Merritt

Thank you to our Patrons

Gigi Nickerson, Amanda Hurst & Coralee Butterfield

ABOUT J.A. ARMITAGE

J.A lives in a total fantasy world (because reality is boring right?) When she's not writing all the crazy fun in her head, she can be found eating cake, designing pretty pictures and hanging upside down from the tallest climbing frame in the local playground while her children look on in embarrassment. She's travelled the world working as everything from a banana picker in Australia to a Pantomime clown, has climbed to the top of Mount Kilimanjaro and the bottom of the Grand Canyon and once gave birth to a surrogate baby for a friend of hers.

She spends way too much time gossiping on facebook and if you want to be part of her Reading Army, where you'll get lots of freebies, exclusive sneak peeks and super secret sales, join up here

https://www.subscribepage.com/v7o8k4

Somehow she finds time to write.

ABOUT ANNE STRYKER

Anne Stryker was born and raised deep in the concrete garden of Jacksonville, Florida. As a Fantasy Romance author, Anne loves crafting fantastical worlds with swoony, humorous, or mysterious male leads and relatable main characters. Embracing the normal in the abnormal is her favorite pastime.

If you'd like to join her in her quest for Happily Ever Afters, you can find her on Instagram or you can join her Faerie Kaleidoscope by signing up to her mailing list:

Instagram: @AuthorAnneStryk
Faerie Kaleidoscope: http://eepurl.com/dGKJ6L

Printed in Great Britain
by Amazon